"Few crime writers, living or dead, have the
language, the ability to effortlessly set a sce
punch, as Jim Nisbet." —Garrett Kenyon, *Spinetingler*

"Nisbet has long been one of crime fiction's best kept secrets."
—Woody Haut, *Crime Time*

"[A] contemporary noir titan." —*Publishers Weekly*

"[A] rock 'n' roll of violence, cruelty, humour, absurdity, psychoanaly-
sis, oneirism, and poetry—is the marque of Jim Nisbet." —*Libération*

"Jim Nisbet is a cult favorite in Europe and it's easy to see why. I've
talked to a few people about this author and comparisons abound;
he's Thomas Pynchon crossed with Raymond Chandler; the
lovechild of Patricia Highsmith and Don DeLillo, and on and on it
goes. For my money I'd say he reads like Jasper Fforde meets Ken
Bruen. One thing for sure, he's unique and man does he have a vivid
imagination." —*SleuthOfBakerStreet.com*

"Jim Nisbet is a poet . . . [who] resembles no other crime fiction
writer. He mixes the irony of Dantesque situations with lyric narration, and achieves a luxuriant cocktail that truly leaves the reader
breathless." —*Drood's Review of Mysteries*

"Jim Nisbet is a lot more than just good . . . powerful, provocative. . . .
Nisbet's style has overtones of Walker Percy's smooth southern
satin, but his characters—losers, grifters, con men—hark back to
the days of James M. Cain's twisted images of morality." —Toronto
Globe and Mail

"Jim Nisbet's work has been tapping directly into the pulse of
America for decades. Like others who have done the same in the past,
it's only later that the rest of us catch up and realize just how right
those trailblazers were all along. That time is now, for all of us to not
only catch up to this unheralded master but to offer him the respect
and regard that he deserves." —Brian Lindenmuth, *Spinetingler*

Snitch World

Jim Nisbet

Snitch World
© Jim Nisbet
This edition © PM Press 2013.

ISBN: 978-1-60486-681-0
Library of Congress Control Number: 2012913629

Cover art by Gent Sturgeon
Cover layout by John Yates
Interior design by briandesign

10 9 8 7 6 5 4 3 2 1

PM Press
PO Box 23912
Oakland, CA 94623
www.pmpress.org

The Green Arcade
1680 Market Street
San Francisco, CA 94102-5949
www.thegreenarcade.com

Printed in the USA , by the Employee Owners of
Thomson-Shore in Dexter, Michigan. www.thomsonshore.com

By the same author:

Baby, just about anywhere you die there's somebody watching. It doesn't make any difference whether they're watching you die in bed or in a chair, somebody is going to be there. It's strictly a spectator sport.

—Eliott Chaze, *Black Wings Has My Angel*

*When it's a man's time to die
God leads him to the perfect place.*

—Frank Herbert, *Dune*

ONE

The Miata jumped the curb and sheared off a light pole. The impact deployed the airbags, but Chainbang was ready. He knifed Klinger's before it was fully inflated and his own before it could crush the glass pipe in his breast pocket. The six-inch blade went through the nylon like a pit bull through a kindergarten.

Or so he thought. His arms absorbing the shocks transmitted by the rim of the steering wheel, Klinger didn't mind a nick on his right cheek inflicted by the blade, its vector skewed by the onrushing fabric. And then, shredding his own safety device, Chainbang stabbed himself too, under the chin.

Neither of them noticed.

The light pole crashed headfirst into the middle of the northbound lanes of Webster and sent a shower of sparks onto the sidewalk. The Miata wound up stalled beyond the opposite side of the median and pointed northbound in the middle of the two southbound lanes.

It was three-thirty in the morning. At the moment, there was no traffic.

Klinger keyed the starter. The solenoid merely clicked. He keyed it again. Same result.

"Fucker's quitting while it's ahead," Chainbang observed.

"Yeah, well," Klinger advocated, "it's quitting while we're behind."

Chainbang beat a tattoo on the lip of the disgorged dash with the blade of his knife. The nearest fire station is only four blocks away, at Turk and Webster. The nearest copshop is just around the corner from the fire station, at Turk and Fillmore.

As Chainbang stared up the street and paradiddled his knife over the vinyl, a swiveling red light came on over the garage door of the fire station.

"Senseless violence," Klinger was saying. He turned the key in the switch like he was turning a screw into a cork. "You think you killed that guy?"

Chainbang shrugged. "I hit him hard as I could."

"Might have done it," Klinger concluded grimly, and now, though he'd been patient with the nonrespondent starter, the shank of the key wrung off in the switch.

That's the thing about adrenaline, Klinger thought, as he thumbed the stub of the key in the darkness adjacent the steering column. A man under its influence doesn't know his own strength.

The preliminary moan of a siren emanated from the rising garage door of San Francisco Fire Station No. 5.

Klinger dropped his hand to the door handle. "It's time for us to go." He held out his other hand. "Give me half of whatever comes out of your pocket."

Chainbang continued to stare through the windscreen, and continued to drum the flat of the knife on what was left of the dashboard. His eyes refocused on the glass in front of him. Now he noticed the long crack that meandered from the lower-right corner of the windscreen on the passenger side to the upper-left corner on the driver's side. It meandered like the Snake River across the befogged reservation of his youth. Befogged is the wrong word. Chainbang's memory of his youth lay beyond any number of smeared thicknesses of graffitied Lexan, securely obfuscated.

The engine of the ladder truck rolled through the

open garage door of the fire station, lights throbbing, siren probing.

Chainbang thought of spearing the beckoning hand to the lid of the center console before he bolted. But, he reflected, word of this minor treachery would inevitably get back to whatever joint he wound up in after this or some other caper, and, shithead or not, nobody, even a Klinger so uniquely snitched out, was entirely without friends.

In that regard was not even he, Chainbang, one of Klinger's friends?

The ladder truck, fully extruded like a pipefish from its den now, aimed many of its lights south toward the Miata, siren in full cry.

"Hey! Wake up! Fork it over!"

Chainbang thrust his free hand into the pocket of his windbreaker and fished up a fistful of bills. Though in the dark he had no idea as to their denomination or quantity, he crushed them into Klinger's waiting palm. "You should invest some of this in driver's education, you fuck."

Klinger didn't waste a moment. His door, being the one that had impacted the light pole, was jammed. So, as they'd been robbing liquor stores with the top down, since they couldn't figure out how to get it up, he tried to step up and out of the stolen sports car with dignity. But the remnants of the airbag entangled his legs, and he and his dignity spilled headlong into the street.

Going to school on Klinger's experience, Chainbang took the time to gleefully lacerate his own airbag to ribbons before he opened the door and stepped onto the landscaped median, formerly home to the ruined light pole.

The fire engine was three blocks away now. From somewhere a little farther away came the distinguishable siren of an ambulance. This would be standard San Francisco emergency response: one or two fire trucks and an ambulance. Not until somebody had determined that a crime had been committed would the cops be called.

East across Webster, beyond the light pole, spread some eight square blocks of housing projects, with which Chainbang was all too familiar. Time was, he might have clambered over one of the entry gates and taken refuge in any of a number of abandoned units, or the various shooting galleries, or a unit known to take in fugitives for a price. In the old days the cops would chase a man to the edge of the projects and stop dead, no matter the hotness of their pursuit, for even the cops were afraid to broach the boundaries of this and other such projects without massive backup, even in broad daylight.

But those days were over. Tonight, Chainbang's better chance was—he cast his mind over the neighborhood—Alamo Square, two blocks straight up Grove Street. He could spend the night burrowed into a clump of Mexican sage the size of a haystack. As long as the cops didn't bring out the dogs, he'd be fine.

He rounded the back of the Miata and put his foot on the prostrate Klinger's chest.

"Hey—what the fuck?"

"Don't follow me, man," Chainbang said. He pointed up the hill. "Go your own way." He pointed toward the projects.

"Don't worry, motherfucker," Klinger said, after a short pause for astonishment. "I done followed you enough for one night."

"You got the gun—right?"

"Gun?" Klinger tried to sit up, but the foot bore down on him. Klinger relaxed. "Last time I saw it, it was on the center console."

Chainbang glanced at the car. One headlight was still functioning, though its beam angled up into the trees further north along the median. The inside of the car was a tangle of darkened nylon.

Two blocks down Webster, at McAllister, the ladder truck erupted in honks of outrage as the SUV of a confused motorist, having entered the intersection despite all the noise and lights, stopped directly in front it.

Two blocks further north, the station's red command vehicle exited the firehouse and turned south, siren blaring and lights flashing.

Lying on his back in the street, Klinger looked up at Chainbang and laughed. "I believe you were the last man to handle the weapon?"

Chainbang scowled and raised the knife.

Klinger threw the fistful of money into Chainbang's face, twisted the knee above the offending foot, and rolled away.

Chainbang fell backward into the Miata with a curse. Klinger found his feet and ran.

Two-thirds up the block toward Fillmore, Klinger heard the squeal of tires and orders, barked over a bumper-mounted PA speaker. Klinger got a grip on his nerves, slowed to a walk, then turned around.

A hundred yards down the hill a black and white blocked the intersection, and in front of the squad car, flooded by headlights and the driver's side spotlight, stood Chainbang, blinking and squinting with his hands up.

Beyond him the totaled Mazda lifted steam into the night.

The paper scattered throughout the intersection had once been, no doubt, legal tender, and might be again. At that distance, Klinger couldn't tell. It might just as well have been calendar pages herded by a breeze through a canyon in a darkened financial district on the last billable day of the year.

Just like most any innocent bystander might do, Klinger stood stock still as the arrest proceeded. He could hear Chainbang's feeble protestations but, at that distance, he couldn't understand what was being said. A cop stood in front of Chainbang shining a flashlight in his face. Another stood behind him, warily, one hand on his holstered service weapon. A third was fitting the bracelets.

One building further up the sidewalk and two stories up, the weights of a double-hung sash rattled in their soffits. "What's up?" a sleepy voice asked.

"Not sure," Klinger replied without turning around. "I thought it was an accident, but there's a lotta cops."

The fire truck finally arrived, and shortly thereafter the commander's red SUV, and then an ambulance, and finally another police car.

"Jeeze," said the man in the window.

"Yeah," Klinger allowed.

"I always wondered," said the man in the window, "why San Francisco always sends two fire trucks and an ambulance to every single fucking 911 call. You know?"

Klinger nodded.

"I mean," the man in the window continued, "that's costing the taxpayer money."

Klinger nodded some more.

"You gotta wonder, what with all these budget shortfalls, closing schools and parks, cutting back on police foot patrols and whatnot, how come they don't just send one truck to a fire, or one ambulance to the shortness of breath, or one cop car to the domestic disturbance. You know?"

Now Chainbang was face down on the hood of the police car, talking over his shoulder as one of the cops, ignoring him, methodically went through his pockets. Surely Chainbang had ditched the knife? And nope. There it was on the trunk lid, its blade still open, just at the edge

8

of a pool of light, with his bandana. The bandana still had a knot in it.

Chainbang like to hold up stores with a bandana tied over his nose and mouth. Like Jesse James and shit, as he liked to say.

"Don't you think?" the man in the window repeated after a moment.

"Yeah," Klinger nodded, as if thoughtfully. "But San Francisco is a wooden city. Used to be, anyway. You get a call for a fire, you just about have to respond with the heavy hand. Hell, it wasn't the earthquake that did in the town, in 1906, it was the fire that raged for days afterwards. They couldn't get up no water pressure, see, and the whole town was built of wood then, so the place went up like Dresden in World War II. Also a wooden city. So was Nagasaki, for that matter. And Saint-Malo."

"The hell you talking about?" the man in the window said.

Klinger frowned. "Combustible cites?"

"Yeah?" The man in the window yawned. "I never heard of any of those places."

Klinger resisted the impulse to confront the only other witness to the crime scene on Webster Street with his own astonishment. "They all burned," was all he said, and he said it as if he were speaking to himself.

The man in the window made no response. Down in the intersection, the investigating officer had extracted a fistful of hastily bundled cash from Chainbang's hip pocket. I thought he pulled that cash from the pocket of his windbreaker, Klinger observed to himself.

"Still," the man in the window started up again. "If only they could do some sort of triage on the original 911 call."

"But they do," Klinger insisted. "You called 911 lately?"

No answer.

Okay, thought Klinger. Either the guy's chickenshit, or he calls 911 all the time and doesn't want me, whom from Adam he knows not, to think he's a snitch. "They ask you now," Klinger said. "What is the nature of your emergency, sir or ma'am as the case may be?"

"Oh," said the man in the window. "They do?"

"But they still send at least one fire truck and an ambulance."

"But why?" insisted the man. "It's expensive."

"Maybe you should go to the meetings," Klinger suggested.

"Like I got time to go to the meetings," the man said tiredly.

Klinger shrugged. "Maybe you could look it up online."

"Man," the man said, "I need to look up what happened to my life online."

You said it, Klinger thought to himself, I didn't.

The window rattled shut.

Down the hill in the intersection, a cop was reading Chainbang his rights. The ladder truck made a U-turn through the intersection and headed back to the station house.

This'll be strike three, Klinger thought, so it wouldn't make much difference if Chainbang snitched me out or not. Things will go hard on him, no matter what. Klinger made a face. He might easily have killed me, and he probably did kill that store clerk. It could well make the difference between life without parole and the hotshot. But Chainbang won't snitch on anybody.

Back to prison, and for what? A hundred bucks? Two hundred?

Klinger had no idea how much money they'd snatched from the cash register, but it made no difference now.

A few yards down the sidewalk a door opened, and a

woman appeared with a dog on a leash. The dog gratefully relieved itself against the trunk of the first tree it came across.

"Hello," the woman said quietly as they moved up the hill. She was young and pretty and nicely dressed.

"Evening," Klinger said. "Nice dog."

"Thank you," the woman said.

Klinger offered the back of his fingers and the dog sniffed them perfunctorily. "Looks like some kind of mix."

"Labradoodle, actually," the woman said.

"Oh? That's a breed?"

The woman nodded and smiled sleepily. "It is now."

"Labrador and poodle, I'd guess."

"That's right."

The dog wagged its tail a little.

"What's her name?"

"His name is Latte."

Klinger blinked first.

"What's going on down there?" she asked.

Klinger looked up from patting Latte's head. Down in the intersection, one cop held open the back door on the black and white. Another cop, holding Chainbang's elbow with one hand, pushed his head down so it would clear the top of the door. Even from that distance, Klinger might have seen that the back door had no handles on the inside. Or maybe he just knew it. "Some kind of accident, I guess."

"It looks as if they are arresting that man. Was he the driver?"

A tow truck arrived, yellow lights flashing, and stopped so as to perfectly obscure Klinger's view of Chainbang. The driver stepped down from the cab of his truck and initiated some paperwork with one of the cops.

"I don't know," Klinger said. "I was walking up the hill, heard a crash and . . ." He shrugged. "I think he took out a streetlight. Next thing I knew, there were many flashing lights down there. They got here really quick."

"Both the fire house and the police station are just up the street. Maybe he's impaired," the girl suggested.

"Could be." Klinger managed a smile. "It's pretty late not to be impaired."

The young woman looked at him. He looked at her. If I had the money, Klinger thought to himself, I damn sure would be impaired. By the look of you, young lady, you can well afford to be impaired and yet, at three-thirty in the morning, you're not. "Just getting home from work?" he ventured.

"Just long enough to freshen up," she nodded, "walk the dog, grab a nap, get back by eight."

"Some kind of deadline," Klinger inferred.

"IPO," the woman told him.

"IPO," Klinger repeated stupidly.

"It's very exciting," she told him. "Nobody knows what's going to happen."

"That's the damn truth," Klinger nodded wearily.

The labradoodle whimpered.

"Latte's gotta go," the woman said. "Nice talking to you."

She turned the dog with his lead and walked quickly down the hill, toward all the lights.

Klinger watched her go, then turned up the hill, where there were no lights.

T W O

Mary Fiducione always took her morning coffee in the little yard behind her studio.

Dexter Gordon's cover of "Don't Explain" quietly interpolated the morning, emanating from a pair of battered speakers screwed to opposite ends of the header above the seven-foot slider, and under the short eave that provided a little protection from the elements. A hummingbird took turns with a fat bumblebee as they both investigated the refulgent trumpets of a datura that towered over the back corner of the little yard. A neighboring ornamental plum, heralding spring only a week ago, now lofted its mauve blossoms above the graying board fence that ran along the north side of the lot.

The weathered table before her was covered by a fading cloth depicting a woman wearing sunglasses, a Jackie O coiffure, and a cocktail dress, surmounting the motto, QUEEN OF FUCKING EVERYTHING. On it lay the *New York Times*, the *Chronicle*, a copy of *The Furies* by Janet Hobhouse, a pot of Scottish breakfast tea, a teaspoon, and a very delicate-looking ceramic cup and saucer decorated with pinkly-tinged cerise tea roses.

But what compelled her interest this morning was the *Idiot's Guide to Programming iPhone Applications*, a scratch pad, a small netbook computer, and her iPhone itself.

The doorbell rang.

Mary frowned and continued to tap at the phone's virtual keyboard.

After a minute, the doorbell rang again.

Mary suddenly remembered that she was expecting UPS to deliver a new belt holster for her phone. Still frowning at the keyboard, she stood up, passed through the open side of the sliding glass door, through the length of the ground floor apartment, and opened the front door.

"Hey," said Klinger.

Mary looked up from her phone, looked back at it, then looked up again. "Are those the sepals of *Salvia leucantha* woven into your hair, or are you just glad to see me?"

Klinger lifted his eyeballs to the tops of their orbits. "If it's the purple parts of Mexican sage you're referring to, yes. Probably."

She looked up again, said, "There's blood on your cheek," and looked back down at the device in her hand.

Klinger touched a fingertip to his cheek and looked at it. "Must have cut myself texting."

With no visible reaction to this quip, Mary held her phone aloft and stepped aside.

Klinger entered. "Checked your mail lately?"

Mary frowned. "It doesn't come until—. Oh." She stepped into the entry hall.

Klinger went straight to the bathroom, closed the door, and relieved himself. Flushing the john and zipping up, he headed into the kitchenette to draw and down, in quick succession, three large glasses of tap water.

"Hydrating so early?" Mary commented, closing the entry door behind her.

Lowering the empty third glass as he swallowed, Klinger nodded with a wordless, weary vigor, and exhaled loudly.

"Nobody about," Mary said simply as she passed him.

Klinger nodded, then sighed so raggedly that his lips flapped. "Cold last night," he said at last. "Foggy, too. Damp. Wet. Miserable."

"You should pick your camping dates a little more rigorously," Mary suggested as she exited the sliding door. "Although, I feel compelled to remind you, there's no such thing as bad weather, only bad gear." Once in the yard, she resumed her seat and waved at an empty chair across the table. "Come in, sit down." She gestured toward Klinger with the phone. "Hungry? Still thirsty?"

"Tired," Klinger said as he passed through the back door. "Worn out. Damp through and through." He took a seat as Dexter Gordon faded to silence. "Unshaven. Unlaundered. On the run. A failure in life."

Mary tapped the screen on the phone. "Whining," said a robotic voice, followed by the very tinny sound of someone scratching out "Beautiful Dreamer" on an out-of-tune violin. "Whining," the phone repeated.

"The fuck?" Klinger blinked.

"Pissed off," the phone said. "Pissed off . . ."

"Mood-identification app." Mary tapped the screen and the phone went silent. "It's been around for maybe two months and already clocked 135,000 downloads."

Klinger exhibited bepuzzlement by lifting a hand and shaking his head.

"Can you multiply nine ninety-five by 135,000?" Mary said impatiently. "I'll give you a hint."

Klinger frowned.

"Round up to ten."

Klinger scowled.

"One million, three hundred and fifty thousand," Mary told him, "is the answer. That's dollars, and that's gross."

Klinger sighed loudly.

"The current arrangement grants the developer a seventy percent royalty against sales. Can you do seventy percent of 1.350×10^6? I'll save you the trouble: 945,000." She held up the phoneless hand. "That's laughably close to one million dollars." She slapped the table so that the teapot, the cup, the saucer, Klinger, and even Janet Hobhouse jumped. "In two months!"

Klinger clasped both hands over his stomach and stared at the ground. "I think I'm about to puke."

Mary ignored him. "And my own sublime app, Aunty Cringle's Guide to California Flora, has been downloaded a miserable thirteen thousand times," she grumbled.

"Yeah?" Klinger's stomach made noises like unto those it might emit if he'd swallowed a vibraslap. "So what's that mean? You made, what, a lousy nine thousand bucks in, what, the two months since you launched your application?"

"Three," Mary corrected him sententiously. "I made nine thousand bucks in three months. What with rent control and socialist health care, I quit my day job two weeks ago," she added proudly.

Klinger frowned. "Were you still at the fortune cookie factory?"

Mary nodded.

"Good on you." Klinger belched sincerely. "Now you'll have the time to get really good at canasta."

Mary sat forward in her chair and spoke in earnest. "You know what the best-selling sensory app is?"

"No," Klinger admitted truthfully.

"You hold up the phone to a person who's belching or farting?"

Klinger frowned suspiciously. "Yeah . . . ?"

Mary nodded. "The phone tells you what the person's been eating."

"You mean you . . . you hold the phone to their mouth or their asshole?" Klinger said incredulously. "Are you serious?"

"As serious as Mahler's Ninth." Mary thumped the table in syncopation with various syllables of the bottom line: "Fourteen million, five hundred thousand downloads."

"What if you've been eating nothing?"

"Fasting?" Mary frowned. "Probably generate a discontinuity," she concluded. "An error code."

Klinger burped, not so quietly. "I'll buy that."

"Well over ten million in royalties," Mary pointed out dreamily.

"Talk about your motherfucking charlatan culture endorsing its own reality," Klinger declared testily. Klinger was beginning to wonder about his stomach. Strange gases were making their way to the surface of the water he'd just consumed, thoroughly acidifying its pH along the way. His stomach hadn't been right since he'd started shitting blood during a drinking binge about . . . Since . . . Klinger frowned. Klinger couldn't remember. Anyway, he'd cut back on his drinking lately, somewhat. Having no money, of course, made cutting back easier. Wrong word. But he was worried that the damage was permanent, which called the bluff on his slow-motion suicide-by-alcohol, which made him nervous.

"Ten million dollars," Mary repeated. "You know what Stendhal said?"

"Fuck no," Klinger replied with certainty.

"He said he'd rather spend fifteen days a month in prison than be forced to converse with the people he saw around him on the street."

"Oh yeah?" Klinger almost smiled.

"Something to that effect."

"And when did he say this?"

Mary considered the question. "I guess by now it must be almost two hundred years ago."

Klinger nodded grimly. "Some things never change."

"So it would seem."

Adjacent to one of the legs of the table, a sow bug stumbled through the grass. Blade by blade, brother. Klinger moved his foot out of its path. "Can this gizmo detect the stink of acetylene on a drunk? Or whatever that byproduct of the metastasis of alcohol and the poor liver's remaining enzymes is?"

Mary shrugged. "I'm not sure." She snapped her fingers. "Maybe that's one you and I could write." She repositioned herself in her chair. "Sure. The phone could tell you how few or many of those enzymes you got left. Maybe scare the bejesus out of a drunk enough to make him reform." She snapped her fingers. "Our app could be the canary in the gold mine."

"For that matter," Klinger said, engaging the jest, "you could turn the phone into a breathalyzer. Guy makes a call, he's too drunk to drive, the phone locks up his car's ignition and calls him a cab." He closed his fist in front of his mouth and contorted his voice. "You're a cab."

Mary looked at Klinger, aghast. "That's fucking brilliant."

"Wait," Klinger said. "Guy gets too drunk to be in public, his phone calls the cops and drops the dime on him. Saves the cops the time and expense of random checkpoints."

"Fucking great!" Mary enthused. "They used to say that the state is best served by silence. But, any time now, the state will be best served by phones!"

"Snitchahol." Klinger laughed in spite of himself. "Now you're talking!" He pointed at Mary: "The iSnitch."

"The iSnitch!" she pointed back. "What an app!"

"We'll make millions!" they said in unison.

After only a little time, their laughter subsided into silence.

Having managed to pierce the morning fog, the sun had begun to warm the yard. The hummingbird whirred overhead. The bumblebee buzzed lazily up and over the fence and out of sight. Klinger, whose every bone ached from his three or four hours of exposure to the elements in Alamo Square Park, not to mention the walk to Mary's from the park, a distance of about two miles, not to mention the impact with the light pole, moved his head, his legs and arms, his every hinged joint, just to feel them creak.

The sow bug had advanced to halfway between the legs on Klinger's side of the table. Klinger wondered what sow bugs eat.

"So," Mary said, not looking up from her phone. "You working these days?"

Klinger gave the sow bug half a smile. "Not so's you'd notice."

Her thumbs busy on the phone, Mary made no response.

Klinger's smile went away. After a minute he repeated himself. "I said, Not so's you'd notice."

"Hm," Mary responded, thumbing the phone. "Need any money?"

Klinger nodded tiredly. "I need money, false identity papers, a car, a dry place to sleep, a steak, and a fifth of whiskey. Even so," he smiled feebly, "I'm a cheap date."

Mary, who had continued to watch her phone while nodding against each item in Klinger's list, now dispensed a definitive half-shake of her head. "I'll give you breakfast and a hundred bucks," she said. "After that, you're on your own. Unless you want to write that app."

"Christ," Klinger said. "If only I wasn't allergic to digging ditches. Then I could feel good about myself."

"They got an app for that," Mary advised him. "It's called a backhoe."

Klinger ran his fingers through his thinning, too-long hair. "What the hell am I gonna do with a hundred bucks?"

"I don't know," Mary said simply. "What were you gonna do without it?"

Klinger considered this. "Starve sober, I guess."

"You haven't done either yet," Mary reminded him.

Klinger diverted his attention from the sow bug long enough to consider Mary. It was hard to credit that, at one time, she and he shared more sex than all the squids in the Pacific Ocean. Subsequently some twenty years had passed without either one of them aware of the existence of the other, even though, with the exception of various stretches Klinger had spent in the Santa Rita jail, and those during which Mary had been touring Europe with some skinny-butted rock star she'd had a kid with, they both lived in San Francisco. Then, early one afternoon, right before it was torn down to make way for condominiums and a shopping mall, they'd run into each other at Japantown Bowl, on Post Street. She was there for the bowling, he was there for the cocktail lounge, both of which were cheap, fun, and open all the time. And just like that they'd fallen into an easy friendship with little to no overt evidence of what might have been much potential baggage. It was a strange eventuality, what they had become. But on the whole it bespoke a genuine affection between them, with no extenuating circumstances to generate confusion.

Plus, neither one of them no longer even so much as thought about cocaine, let alone consumed it.

Coincidence?

Klinger smiled and looked down. The sow bug had disappeared.

Who the hell knew? Who understood? Who could even remember, much less keep track of it all?

Not Klinger.

In the interim, while Mary Fiducione worked her way through the rock star, parenthood, her first two or three businesses, and finally an apprenticeship in "botanicals" under an acknowledged and much-published expert in the field, Klinger had maintained himself within San Francisco's asteroid belt of petty crime and criminals, never approaching too close to the warmth of the sun shed by the big score, never straying too far into the gelid outer reaches of the prison system.

Last night was an exception, he reminded himself hopefully. Chainbang, who had done plenty of time in real joints, long enough for his real moniker, Chang Yin Winter Horse, to have permanently metastasized into his nickname, was (a) not supposed to be in possession of a gun, being a felon and all, and (b) not supposed to have bashed that convenience store clerk on the side of his head with a frozen whole chicken. It was bad enough Klinger was hanging out with Chainbang at all; totally over his head, in fact. Chainbang had a theory, which was, either a man evolved at the expense of society, or it was going to be the other way around. Not that Chainbang could articulate this idea; but Chainbang had advanced far down a path illuminated by its and his own lights. And now there seemed to be a, er, uh, shadow, that was it, a shadow hovering over, nay, blighting his existence as a result.

"Put your clothes in the washer," Mary told him, still not looking up from her phone. "Take two ibuprofen and have a bath. There's a box of epsom salts under the sink. Use two cups. Take your time. I'll rotate your stuff into the dyer. There's an Italian place around the corner on Chestnut Street that's open for lunch. Little booths, excellent wines, only jazz on the sound system. It's on me." She tapped the face of the phone, dropped it onto the table cloth, stretched her arms, and yawned.

"Then you're out of here," she concluded with a sleepy smile.

THREE

When Klinger hit the door of the Hawse Hole, he had $120 in his pocket.

A couple drinks to take the edge off, he was thinking, then a good night's sleep at the Tuolumne Meadows Residential Hotel, which was right upstairs, where he could put down the C-note against a week's rent.

The well vodka was a Chinese brand he'd never heard of, but three dollars got you a good pour, and it was 100 proof.

"Can't see how you can drink that shit," said an old man seated two stools down from Klinger. "Ain't fit for motor grader coolant."

"Tastes pretty cool to me," Klinger affably stipulated. "But you wait right there while I double-check." Klinger assayed a second and then a third sip, each less dainty than the one preceding it. "Ahhhh," he allowed, carefully centering the empty nervous glass on its coaster. "Cool as can be."

"Cool as October punkins in a frosty moonlit field, I guess," the old man obliged.

Klinger shook his head. "I've never seen a pumpkin in a field by day or by night. Though I have," he added truthfully, "been frosted upon." He turned the glass between his fingers reflectively.

"Easy does it," his neighbor concluded.

"That's about the size of it," Klinger agreed.

"You like to savor it," the old man reasoned, "or you're too broke to do it right."

"Right in two."

"Hit us again," the old man told the bartender.

The bartender did as he was bade.

"Thanks." Klinger toasted the old man with his freshened drink.

The old man nodded. "Minds me of a famous singer/songwriter/guitarist I seen once, up there in Bolinas. You know Bolinas?"

"Heard of it," Klinger nodded. "Up the coast a ways."

"It's thirty miles," the old man said. "And you never been there?"

Klinger shook his head.

"You oughta go sometime," the old man suggested. "They got trees and beaches and shit."

"Yeah?" said Klinger, evincing no interest whatsoever.

"Anyway," the old man continued, "this singer/songwriter/guitarist guy had spent many a year practicing to be an alcoholic, as he himself put it. Got pretty good at it, too, as he himself put it. One thing, though, drunk as he got? He could still play the guitar, and he'd never buzz a string." The old man took a sip of his own drink. "It's about enough to piss a man off."

"You play?" Klinger thought to ask, as he realized that the fluttering on the surface of his drink was the reflection of the blades of a ceiling fan, and not his optic nerve shorting out.

"Not so's you'd notice," the old man said. "I had the classic problem."

Klinger raised an eyebrow. "And which classic problem was that?"

"I'm straying from my original story—."

Klinger lifted both thumbs without losing his grip on his glass. "I got all day."

The old man nodded. "I'm minded of another guy, who announced to his momma, one fine morning, when he was about nine years old, that he wanted to be a musician when he grew up. Well now, son, his momma replied, that's all fine and dandy, but you can't do both."

Klinger affected half a smile. "I like her."

"Me, too," the old man agreed.

"You know her?"

The old man nodded.

"So what happened?"

"I grew up."

"And the music?"

"Had to put it down. Children to raise, food to put on the table, wife to look after, job to attend to. Like that."

"Uh . . ." Klinger said, temporarily at a loss. "Well? You probably got grandchildren."

The old man assumed a thousand-yard stare and shook his head. "Not so's you'd notice."

Why am I drinking in this dump and acting surprised that I'm talking to a human train wreck instead of the president of Hewlett Packard? Klinger wondered to himself. He took a sip of vodka. The ice had gotten to it by now, diluting it slightly, but chilling it too. He had another sip.

"So," Klinger said aloud, setting down his glass, "you spent your whole life taking care of a family that blew up or died off or disappeared somehow, and in any case left you with nothing but a guitar, in a case under the bed, that you no longer remember how to play?"

Abruptly, Klinger fixed his gaze on his drink. Every once in a while he'd get in a mood and find himself making aggressive remarks to perfect strangers which proclivity generated at least a fifty-fifty chance of fetching him a beer bottle upside his head as opposed to witnessing a fit of convulsive weeping, and he had scars where the hair had never grown back to prove it. Today, however . . .

"Something like that," the old man said simply.

"Shit." Klinger said gruffly. "I'll bet you can play the chromatic bejesus out of a guitar."

The old man shook his head. "Not really."

Klinger slipped each of his hands palm down on the barstool, each under its respective thigh, and stared at his drink. "Anyway," he said, "we were talking about a musician who was practicing to be an alcoholic."

The old man nodded. "Indeed we were." He lifted his glass and found it empty. "Damn," he said.

"Hit us again," Klinger said.

"Thanks," the old man said, as the bartender covered the ice in the old man's glass with Jameson.

"What kind of Irish is in the well?" Klinger asked hopefully.

"Standing Stone," the bartender said. "Guaranteed to be the death of you."

"Says so right on the label," the old man said.

Klinger nodded.

"How about it, amigo?" the bartender asked him.

"Sure." Klinger freed his right hand and downed his vodka.

"Don't know how you can drink that shit," the old man said, as he watched the bartender dispense a generous pour of whiskey into a fresh glass. "You'll be shitting blood in the morning."

"You were telling me a story," Klinger said.

"So I was. Singer/songwriter/guitarist is sitting on a stool in the bar, facing an audience. He's completely drunk. There's a shot glass brimful of tequila sitting dead center on a second stool, right next to him, directly below the peghead of his beautiful big-body D-35 Martin, a guitar he's managed to hang onto his whole life."

"How old is this guy?"

"Seventy if he's a day."

"Damn," admitted Klinger.

"Not sure how he made it." The old man looked at his whiskey. It had always amazed Klinger how some people could let a drink just sit in front of them for what invariably seemed an eternity. "So he's rambling, this guy. He's got on the ten-gallon hat, the concho belt, the brush-popper shirt with nacre buttons, a duster, boot-cut jeans, and riding-heel cowboy boots. It's raining outside. Do you remember when it used to rain in California?"

Klinger nodded. "I do."

"Special, wasn't it?"

"Very."

"Every year, regular as clockwork, Mother Nature would show up in late October, early November, Thanksgiving at the latest . . ." The old man swept one hand at arm's length over the bar to his right, then repeated the gesture to his left. ". . . and wash away six months of piss and dogshit and good intentions. Just wash them away."

Klinger nodded. "And sin." He nodded again.

The old man lifted his glass. "And sin, brother."

They toasted and drank.

"So every now and again, while this guy is telling this goddamn endless story, he'd reach over and pluck up the shot glass with two fingers, like this. And he'd lift it over the peghead of the guitar and around the shoulder strap and take a sip, like this." The old man demonstrated the move. "Then he'd put it back, dead center on the second stool. And the whole time he'd never take his eyes off the audience. Not once. By and by," he continued, as he set down his own drink, "the tequila was gone. But the goddamn story continued. Two or three times he'd reach over for the glass, never taking his eyes off the audience, lift it to his lips, find it was empty, betray not a whit about the discovery, set the glass back down again, and go on with his goddamn story."

"What was this story about, anyway?" Klinger thought to ask.

"The good old days in Greenwich Village. Is there some other subject?"

"I don't know." Klinger looked at him. "Never been there."

"Well, see? What do you know?" the old man nodded. "By and by, some friend of this guitarist sneaks up behind him and takes the glass, thinking to help him out by fetching a refill."

"Now there's a friend."

"A woman, actually," the old man recollected. "Pretty thing."

"It's always a woman."

"There's a lot to that not growing up stuff," the old man agreed. "More than meets the eye."

"Sounds to me like it's nothing but what meets the eye."

"There's a point in there somewhere, I'm sure," the old man said, somewhat frostily.

"My point exactly," Klinger replied pointedly.

"But the bartender," the old man persevered, "who is annoyed that his musical evening is turning into a therapy session run by a drunk, tells the young lady that her friend is cut off until he takes the trouble to do what he's being paid to do, which is sing and play the songs for which he's famous and which changed the world for the better back when we was all hippies."

"Speak for yourself," Klinger advised him tartly.

"I am," said the old man. "So, naturally, she waits. By and by . . ." The old man snapped his fingers. They didn't quite snap, so he snapped them a second time. "Our guitarist does it again."

"He reaches over—."

"—and makes as if to pinch up the shot glass."

"But the shot glass isn't there."

"He doesn't turn a hair."

"I'll bet he twitched internally."

"Actually, the twitch was quite visible."

"Didn't he look over at the second stool, just the least glance, to make sure he hadn't missed?"

"Nope. He knew it wasn't there. So, he draped the unemployed hand on the neck of his guitar and went back to his story."

"This sounds excruciating," Klinger said.

"It was that," the old man agreed, "but it was raining too hard to leave gracefully."

"So . . ."

"So, by and by, he does it again."

"He reaches over—."

"—And makes as if to pinch up the shot glass between thumb and middle finger."

"Which still isn't there."

"Which he had forgotten."

"Or was expecting to arrive at any moment."

"Either way, we had to watch him repeat this performance three or four times before somebody finally yelled out for him to shut up and play us a tune. That's when it got pathetic."

"It's been sounding pathetic to me for some time."

"'I can't,' the guitarist told us, and he clasped his picking hand to his throat. 'I'm parched.'"

Klinger had no snappy retort for this.

"A silence descended on the whole room," the old man said. "There was fifteen or twenty people packed in there, not counting a pool table, but at that moment you could hear a burrito going round and round in the microwave behind the bar."

"Pretty quiet," Klinger allowed.

"The bartender relented and the girl delivered our guitarist his shot. He made a point of downing it in one go. Then he set the empty down, dead center on the stool, and proceeded to play and sing the prettiest, saddest, loneliest ballad you ever heard. He wrote it, too. And he buzzed not a string, forgot not a lyric. He even yodeled at the end. Real plaintive."

Klinger and the old man weren't the only people in the present-tense barroom, but now a silence descended over this one, too.

"It was enough to tear your heart out. Two or three women in the crowd started cryin'. I'm not makin' this up. When he finished, the damn bartender bought a round on the house."

"If I pulled a stunt like that," the present-tense bartender declared, "I'd be out on the street with the rest of you bums."

"But we'd be brothers," the old man suggested.

"Until the time came for the next drink," the bartender suggested.

"All of about fifteen minutes," the old man agreed.

"Brotherhood is volatile," Klinger observed, thinking the while of Chainbang's attempt to cheat him out of his cut. "Say," Klinger said aloud, "anybody seen today's *Chronicle*?"

"There's one right here," the bartender said, handing one over the bar. "No Sports Section."

"Organized sports pave the road to fascism," the old man said.

Klinger frowned. "Haven't I read that somewhere?"

The old man looked at Klinger, then shook his head. "I seriously fucking doubt it."

Klinger quickly perused the Metro section. He found no mention of a liquor store clerk getting himself killed in the course of a robbery. Nor of a subsequent arrest in the middle of Webster Street. This brightened Klinger's outlook considerably. "Say," he said, "how about another round?"

The bartender poured. "This one's on me. That was a good story."

"Well I'll be damned," Klinger said, genuinely touched. "Thanks."

"It's that kinda joint," the old man said, not without satisfaction. "So what if it's in the Tenderloin?"

"So," said Klinger, after the first sip of his fourth drink. "What happened to that genius old drunk, anyway?"

The old man regarded the shimmer atop his refreshed whiskey. "He quit drinking," he finally said.

"Really?" said Klinger.

"Really?" said the bartender.

"Yep," the old man affirmed. He lifted his glass and toasted the room. "Then he died."

FOUR

It's like some monotheistic entity damned me to a thousand years of insomnia, Klinger thought, just to demonstrate that he has the juice. There can be no other reason. I'm just not important enough to—. I've got to get some sleep.

After any number of convivialities, free drinks, matched rounds, spillage, and forgotten knee-jerk quaffs, Klinger got out of the bar with $57.32 of the $120 he'd entered with, as drunk as a man of high rank in a feudal society, which he was not.

Out the front door of the Hawse Hole a racetrack turn launched him up one flight of stairs into the lobby of the Tuolumne Meadows Residential Hotel. Against a blown-up backdrop of a Hetch Hetchy Valley photographed before the O'Shaughnessy Dam turned it into a reservoir in 1923, five years after the hotel itself was subdivided into ten by twelve rooms intended to accommodate merchant seamen returning from World War I, a sleepy clerk took $51.42 cash up front for three nights' stay, leaving Klinger with $5.89 mad money, in exchange for which he received a key bound by a beaded chain to a plastic one-inch fisherman's anchor.

"Up three flights, take the hall to your left, Room 335. The moaner two doors down is a permanent resident, so I don't wanna hear about it."

Klinger stared at the key. "Three-thirty-five," he repeated. His breath came with some difficulty and not a little audibly.

Having resumed his seat behind the counter, the clerk took up a large pair of tailor's shears. "Right in one." Without sparing another glance for Klinger, he resumed his close perusal of a celebrity magazine, open on the desk before him.

"Moaner," Klinger repeated. "Moaner . . ."

"He doesn't go on all night, as a rule," the clerk said, as the twin blades of his shears carefully limned a starlet's gam. He moved the back of his head toward a clock on the wall behind him, which had twelve Chinese ideograms on its face. "It's already late."

"Already late," Klinger repeated stupidly. Existentially, as he might have enunciated if he possessed breath sufficient to the task, it's never been so Late as it is Now. If I just had another drink . . .

"Run along," the clerk suggested. The tips of his shears nipped the image of the actress just between arm and ribcage.

Run, Klinger was thinking to himself, as he bounced off the farther wall of the stairwell. As if with languor he arrested his rebound by clinging to the banister with both hands. *Run home.*

The room, once achieved, seemed hardly worth the effort. There was a window, nailed shut. There was a radiator, cold as a dead man's armor. If they ever find the entropic core of the universe, Klinger mused, it's going to turn out to be a lump of cast iron beneath a window that can't be opened, and I'll be in there with it. The floor had been carpeted wall to wall a long time ago, but now its polyester fibers yearned an inch or two into the foetid troposphere like hairs in the mouth of a feeding anemone—Take it easy, Klinger told himself, it's just threadbare carpet. Merely sordid. Nothing new. Nothing terrible. Plus it's dry in here. There's a roof. There's a lock on the door . . .

A moan came through the wall. A cry between unheard sobs, maybe. Nothing out of the ordinary.

The bedding appeared to be clean, a small miracle, until he peeled back the blanket to discover an uncommonly long pubic hair dead center on the sheet. Flicked by thumb and forefinger, the hair scampered across the sheet and disappeared over the far edge.

As if possessed by a suicidal animation, that hair, thought Klinger, and he proceeded to get lost and found in his own shirt. I like that. I endorse suicidal animation.

The pillow smelled like the driver's seat in the oldest bus in the transcontinental fleet, but Klinger hit it face down and paid the odor no mind. With suicidal animation his sense of collective identity fled in the wake of the multi-cornered hair, over the edge of consciousness and into the seething abyss of the universal, non-internet id.

Wherein, though it be a mere blighted star in a galaxy of predominant neuropathies, every mind continues to twinkle. In this case the mind of Klinger ginned up a full-blown parable complete with sights, sounds, smells—altogether haunting tactilities, to wit:

Chainbang, spawn of Amerindian-Chinese ancestry, convinces Klinger that if they could scare up the means to score a pair of bus tickets to Leadville, Colorado, they could make their fortunes.

"My forbears all had shovel teeth," Chang Yin tells him, opening his mouth. "Put your fingers in my mouth—here. Touch the roof behind the incisors." Klinger does so. The two top incisors launch backward into Chang Yin's mouth like upside down water slides. "Melungeon tri-racial isolate," Chang Yin says around Klinger's fingers. "Could be Mongolian, could be Choctaw, hey—," he snatches Klinger's wrist, pulling the fingers out of his mouth and twists. "Could be miscegenatin' Appalachian peckerwood."

"Okay, okay . . ." says Klinger. "The fuck difference . . . this swarm . . ." He bats the air in front of his face.

After a lot of fooling around which consumes a molar volume of oneiric neurons, Chainbang reverts to his given name of Chang Yin for the purposes of this venture and perhaps in order to evade detection by Interpol, as he and Klinger materialize down the three front steps of a mystical Greyhound bus eastbound from Salt Lake City—picks, headlamps, thermal underwear, hickory shirts, gum boots, and galluses all packed into army surplus rucksacks, canteens and enameled cups clanking—in front of the snowbound US Post Office in Leadville, Colorado.

No hotel, no steak and eggs breakfast, no nervous glass of whiskey populate the dream—its hapless denizens go straight to work. The portal to which is a cutbank below Highway 24, a quarter mile south of the town limits. Chang Yin knows the way. Chang Yin's ancestors on his father's side had been imported to Leadville and the surrounding areas to dig the mines, as they had throughout the developing West in the nineteenth century, to dig for gold, silver, and many other minerals—the largest molybdenum mine in the western hemisphere is just a few miles north of Leadville—and these ancestors had handed down to select progeny their knowledge of the local mines, tunnels, claims, discoveries—and lost treasures, of course—all of which is explained to Klinger in a single intense packet burst of simultaneous awareness.

In their zeal for discovery and for the freedom rumored to be purchasable with cold cash, Chang Yin's ancestors secretly honeycombed all the hills surrounding any meaningful claim or strike throughout the mineral West, Leadville prime among them. The town and its surrounding hills are a warren of impromptu tunnels and exploratory digs, as any number of collapsed carport slabs, well bores, and septic tank excavations regularly attest. Few if any of these burrowings were properly shored. Many of them are partially or completely caved in. It is illegal to enter them and it is illegal to remove any material from them—not because anybody cares whether autonomous miners die or not, but because somebody owns every cubic inch of mineral rights for as far as the eye can or cannot see, whether they trouble to exploit these rights or not.

But that didn't stop Chang Yin's father and his father's best friend, one Steamboat Burton, from the odd underground foray, and, though nobody ever explicitly stated as much, rarely had they not returned with a nugget or two sufficient to ease the family through the next couple of frigid months above ground. This was the knowledge that Chang Yin Sr. had passed on to Chang Yin Jr. Here is the entrance, son. Here is what a nugget looks like in the wild. There's always one around that other people have missed if you know what to look for. Only Chinese people have the nerve to go into these tunnels, and there's not so many of us around here anymore. Don't tell anybody what I've told you, and, always remember, respect the earth, wear a helmet, carry extra batteries, don't go alone, and don't go too deep.

Brush and rubble effortlessly cleared, Klinger follows Chang Yin into a tunnel.

The first thing Klinger notices is the change in weather. Outside, all is windblown snow. Conditions are so lousy there isn't even any traffic on Highway 24. Before they manage to instantaneously clear the debris, the road is completely drifted over. A complete whiteout.

A hundred yards inside the gallery, however, there's a mere draft and it's dank but, while chilly, it's not freezing. To their knowledge nobody has been this way in many years but the smell of freshly dug earth permeates the air, rank and foetid and not unlike . . . rotten carpet . . .

Klinger frowns but does not awaken. His eyelids, though twitching, remain closed. The continuum of oneiric greed unreels, uninterrupted.

The tunnel slopes sharply down. It narrows, too, and they often stop to clear debris sufficient to allow a man to pass. Here and there a rotted timber has splintered, pushed by the insistent geology behind or above it. Only occasionally, and that by aiming his headlamp upward, does Klinger discern a lintel or any kind of overhead shoring timber, and all of these timbers, posts or lintels, appear to be creosoted rail ties, whole or fractioned, and he wonders about the condition of the local railroad.

The height of a tunnel never exceeds seven feet, more or less the vertical height of a railroad tie with one to two feet of its length buried. Never is a tunnel more than three feet wide. Often these dimensions are much less, and the two men have to crawl on their sides in single file to make progress. Because of these narrow confines, their picks and shovels are short-handled.

At the first fork in the tunnel, Chang Yin takes a confident left. At the next fork, ten minutes later, he takes another left.

Klinger tries to remember these turns. He tells himself that, on his the way back, after a cave-in has killed Chang Yin, a left will be a right. And this determination soothes his confidence until, turning to heave a shovelful of gravel, his headlamp reveals, much to his surprise, a tunnel that forks to the right behind him. He'd crouched past this gallery, as they are called, without noticing it. Surely, encountered on the way back, this gallery would count as a right turn, and . . . And what? Would it eventually join a tunnel that made its way to the surface? Or not?

"Klinger, mon," Chang Yin says, behind him now, "watch out for the hole."

Klinger turns. Chang Yin is facing him, his headlamp aimed downward and into a hole that disappears into darkness between them.

Chang Yin shows Klinger a stone and holds a finger to his lips.

Chang Yin drops the stone into the hole.

A silence wells between them like a dead spot on an FM dial.

They never hear from the stone again.

"Surely," Klinger says, "the fucker found bottom somewhere?"

"Hard to say, mon," Chang Yin says simply. He offers Klinger a hand. "I ain't been down there." He smiles. "No long rope."

"You would," Klinger says, as he floats a hand as if weightlessly over the hole, "explore it if you had a long rope?"

"One thing's for sure around here." Chang Yin turns his back and clambers over a pile of tailings. "The more fucked up a place appears to be, the fewer the people who have checked it out. Put another way, one man's agonizing death is another man's golden opportunity."

"Golden," Klinger concludes. And the thought refreshes his attitude.

"Golden," Chang Yin affirms.

Not a few twists and turns later, Chang Yin stops for a breather. He offers Klinger his canteen.

Klinger frowns in his sleep.

"That tastes like water," Klinger says in the dream.

"It is water," Chang Yin tells him.

Klinger expresses astonishment. "A man goes through all this shit, and all you can offer him is water?"

"If a man goes through all this shit and finds a little gold, he can buy all the whiskey he wants," says Chang Yin.

"Later. Right now," he points along the beam of his headlamp, "a man wants his faculties about him. Anything can happen."

Klinger doesn't ask Chang Yin what that means.

They come to another fork.

"Hmmm," Chang Yin says. "Let's reconnoiter."

"What, you got a GPS?" Klinger quips.

"GPS doesn't work down here," Chang Yin replies.

"You've tried?"

"Sure. But even if it did work, it couldn't tell you which way to go. Hell, these tunnels?" When Chang Yin shakes his head, the beam of his headlamp oscillates along the glistening walls. "They go everywhere. My ancestors were so crazy for gold, they'd dig parallel tunnels just a few yards apart, with just enough dirt and rocks between them to keep them from caving in. Sometimes they'd tunnel right through the side of another man's tunnel, and the whole thing would cave in. If everybody survived they'd apologize to one another, fold their hands together and bow and shit, then they'd tunnel off in opposite directions. They were crazy for gold. Funny, too."

"Anybody ever get rich?" While this seems an obvious question to have asked before they ever boarded the bus in Salt Lake City—well, here they were, weren't they.

"Once in a while, I'm told, a man would come up out of one of these tunnels and go home, get cleaned up, get on the bus to Denver, and disappear forever. These guys weren't exactly communicative. Sure they had partners. It's a lot of work to dig these things. And can you imagine? They'd dig five or six days a week for a legitimate mine, then come out here and go right back at it in their spare time. Nights, Sundays, whenever. Talk about ambition."

"Yeah," Klinger repeats without enthusiasm. "Ambition."

"If a guy made a real strike, nobody would ever hear

about it. Most of them were like my daddy and Steamboat. They'd tunnel when nobody else was around, or in places that were already played out, or places where everybody else was sure there were no trace minerals, or places deemed too dangerous. Daddy and Steamboat always said the best place to look was where everybody else had already given up. What looks worthless to a mining company with thousands or hundreds of thousands in overhead might look real good to one or two guys with cheap rent and a couple of kids to feed."

After a quarter of a mile that Klinger was certain had taken them in a complete circle—"Following trace," Chang Yin called it—Chang Yin pauses. "Hmmm." He looks around. From the bib pocket of his overalls he pulls his father's hand-drawn map and lays it on an angle of repose of dirt and stones that fitfully trickles around both sides of a shoring post. He studies it. He turns it ninety degrees to its previous position. He brushes aside dirt and studies some more. He turns the map thirty-five degrees, traces a fingertip over it, stops. "Hmmm."

Klinger's headlamp dims to half its previous intensity. "Uh-oh." It brightens again.

From the back pocket of his bib overalls Chang Yin produces a gas-station map of Colorado, unfolds it, lays it atop the first one. "North." He touches an X scratched into the shoring timber. "Dead north."

Klinger stares in amazement. "How do you know that?"

Chang Yin grins. "They prairie-dogged."

"They—what?"

Chang Yin raises a finger. "You dig straight up till you breach the surface. Have a look around, maybe even bring out the compass. Then you drag a bunch of brush over the hole, come back down, leave a mark or a sign." He folds up the maps. "And dig on. Let's go."

Klinger follows Chang Yin while the latter counts footsteps, heel to toe. The ceiling gets a little higher here, and it feels as if the floor has leveled off, though it is hard to tell. Now the tunnel widens and the shoring timbers become more frequent. Chang Yin sets his maps down on the floor and studies them. Then he looks up at the ceiling. "We're close," he says. "Help me." And he begins to hack at the tunnel ceiling with his pick. Klinger joins him. Dirt falls into their faces. Rocks, too. "What the fuck are we doing?" Klinger says aloud. "Animatedly committing suicide?"

"Keep digging," Chang Yin tells him.

Soon enough, Klinger's pick strikes something different.

"That's it," Chang Yin says. "Hit it!"

Klinger hits it. Splinters come away with the clods from the ceiling. Wood.

"Isn't this a little bit dangerous?" Klinger yells above the clatter of material.

Chang Yin hacks at the roof too. "Keep digging!" And then, just as Klinger feared, the roof of the tunnel gives way.

Klinger looks down to avoid the cascade of dirt and stones. Expecting suffocation, he holds his breath. Into the circle of light at his feet tumbles a human skull.

"Holy shit!" Klinger straightens up with such alacrity that his helmet crashes through the rotted roof, foul bones and scraps of cloth shower and drape upon him, and strange cool particles trickle between his collar and his tingling nape.

Chang Yin is laughing, and laughing hard. A minute passes before he can coherently blurt, "We're under the cemetery!" and he dissolves into laughter again. "Oh, man," he manages to add, "you should have seen your face."

"One man's roof is the floor of another man's coffin," Klinger realizes, in a succinct deployment of dream logic. "A fucking coffin!"

Bits of flesh still cling to the skull. Horrified at least as much as he's disgusted, Klinger punts it into the darkness with a shout. "Nuggets of gold, my ass!"

"See!" Chang Yin extends his arm. His headlamp illuminates the tunnel beyond, which runs straight, level and true. Fifty yards along, as Chang Yin explains, a gallery transects their tunnel, connecting to a parallel tunnel, which, in its turn, runs below the next parallel row of graves in the town cemetery.

"Gold nuggets, my ass," Klinger whispers aloud.

"A gold watch will do!" Chang Yin crows. He's on his hands and knees, the better to rake through the bones, cloth, and pine splinters with his bare hands. "A pearl necklace! A hand mirror from the nineteenth century! A gold piece tucked into a waistcoat pocket with which to pay the ferryman!"

"Gold nuggets my ass," Klinger whispers. His voice, hoarse with hopelessness, pushes a plume of condensation before it, into the frigid air of the hotel room.

"Gold nuggets my ass, gold nuggets my ass . . ."

FIVE

Klinger faced the day as if it were a firing squad.

How would that be, exactly?

First, recounting the $5.89 in his jeans, he realized that he had the price of a cup of coffee and a doughnut, maybe, but, unlike almost everybody else around him in the street, he certainly couldn't afford a cappuccino and a chocolate croissant. As go firing squads, this eroded his dignity.

When he'd first come to San Francisco, in the latter third of the 20th century, Klinger felt entirely at home. He turned up in early fall wearing a hickory shirt and jeans over long johns, and wool socks within a knackered pair of cork boots. He'd left his ten-gallon straw hat behind the seat of a hay truck whose driver woke him up in time to drop him off at the 505 feeder to I-80 West, just south of Wycoff, California. The guy had picked him up in Weed, allowing for the first continuous four hours of sleep since he crossed the border at Grand Forks, British Columbia— about 800 miles and a week before.

But the point was, at that moment, dressed as he was, broke and alone, he'd never felt like he belonged someplace like he felt he belonged in San Francisco. People smiled at him on the street. In Washington Square Park two hours later, Klinger was sitting on a southwest-facing bench in the northeast corner of the park, his eyes closed against the afternoon sun. A guy sat down next him. Klinger didn't open his eyes. The guy asked where he was coming from. A logging camp about two hundred miles north of Spokane, Klinger told him, still not opening his eyes, north of the Idaho panhandle. What brings you to San Francisco. I heard it was a nice place. The damn truth, the man said. People seem to want to talk to you here, Klinger ventured. I first came here in a boxcar, the man said, in 1929. Klinger opened his eyes. The sunlight was brilliant, and he blinked and squinted. Didn't have a red cent, the man continued, and that didn't make a bit of difference to the first two or three hundred people I met. Klinger turned for a look. The guy had on a blue blazer with gold buttons, a red silk pocket square, white duck trousers, blue socks and a pair of tasseled black loafers. Met a guy called Harry Bridges. Ever hear of him? Can't say as I have. One of the founders of the ILWU. ILWU . . . ? International Longshore and Warehouse Union, the man patiently explained. Then he chuckled. Damndest Australian you could ever hope to meet. Anyway, he found me a job on the docks. Later, we got our heads busted, did a little jail time together, and pissed off Joe McCarthy. A few years after the war, with a wife and a third kid on the way, I got into advertising. The man smiled at a pigeon nodding its way through a circle on the sidewalk in front of the bench. The money was better, but it was nowhere near as much fun. Now I'm retired. He sighed. Been retired. My wife parks me here every morning for an hour to take the sun while she attends her Tai Chi class. San Francisco's been good to me. He held out his hand. Name's Jimmy. Klinger returned the handshake. Hungry? Klinger nodded. Let's go. The man stood slowly. There's a good breakfast on the other side of Columbus— although, he winked, this being North Beach, you can get an argument about every word in that sentence.

Jimmy bought him breakfast. Not even to hear his story, did Jimmy buy him breakfast, though he got some of that. No, Jimmy told Klinger, as they shook hands and parted, never to meet again, it was a pleasure to watch a hungry man eat.

And where the fuck is Jimmy this morning, Klinger muttered, trembling on the chilly street. Deceased way less than half the time between then and now, no doubt, he scowled. Even Jimmy's kids are probably dead by now, and maybe I'm the only man in this town that remembers him. What kind of a fucking human being am I? Did I ever help a guy out like he helped me? How can I help other people if I can't even help myself? Now there's a reason for self-improvement. Or an excuse for devolution. That logging camp might have been the last honest work I ever did. He squinted. I can't remember.

Back to the firing squad. Two days and six bucks to go. Carry-out destiny. Always round up, if you're feeling pessimistic, and round down if you're feeling otherwise, a meager dichotomy that leaves me pincered between five and six bucks. Klinger exhales sufficiently to flap his lips. I must have helped somebody, Klinger self-remonstrated as he shuffled up the sidewalk, with a buck, a meal, a pack of smokes, a bag of chips, a garbage bag to use as a rain suit—something, sometime, one thing, once at least. Yes? No?

A man passing the other way delivered a blow to the trunk of his torso with a magnitude considerably greater than a jostle.

"The fuck you watch where you—," Klinger rebounded, both hands snatched from their pockets and ready to pound his impotent despond into the frame of the other, no matter the circumstance.

"Tsk," leered the other man, fashioning his several yellowed teeth into a close-up portrait of a window through which somebody has heaved a chair. "Kinda touchy for eight-thirty in the ayem, ain't we?"

Klinger's vehemence, despite its being so suddenly uncorked, allowed for a moment's pause, which allowed him to recognize his interloper before he punched him. "Frankie," Klinger replied, surprised, but not so surprised as to forego appending "Geeze," Frankie's street moniker. They clasped hands, though not in the handshake known and employed throughout the developed nations, but each by lacing the knuckles of the right hand with the other's as if grasping the handle on a stein of beer.

"Frankie," Klinger greeted him, "What the hell are you up to?"

"Oh," Frankie replied easily, "about a hundred a day."

It was a joke and Klinger laughed. But then, he squinted, giving Frankie the once-over, the joke may well also be the truth. "When did you get out?"

Frankie shrugged.

"Clear?"

Frankie shook his head. "Parole."

"Does that mean you're not supposed to be talking to me?"

Frankie shrugged. "You never did no hard time—did you?"

"Nah," Klinger admitted. And, though it diminished his status with the likes of Frankie and Chainbang, he didn't mind admitting it. Indeed, status with the likes of these guys seemed a very small price to pay for a dearth of prison time. Very small.

"So let's hang," Frankie smiled.

Oh joy, Klinger said to himself.

"Care for a drink?"

Klinger brightened. Frankie was the odd hophead who didn't mind alcohol. Klinger could worry about the future later. "I care for a drink," he said.

"Know a place a man can smoke, too?"

Which is how they wound up on adjacent stools at the Hawse Hole at 9:35 in the morning.

"Excellent," Frankie assayed, looking around.

"Joint closes at two in the ayem and reopens four point five hours later."

"Half-hour after the sugar kicks in," Frankie surmised, not without a hint of admiration. "Gives a man time to drag a comb over his head."

"Ya gotta think they know their client base," Klinger agreed.

The bartender swabbed the plank between them. "What's your pleasure, gents?"

Frankie gestured politely.

"You holding?" Klinger asked frankly.

Frankie laid a twenty on the bar.

"Hot coffee with cream and sugar and a double-shot of Jameson," Klinger said without hesitation.

"You want the Jameson back or—," the bartender started to ask.

"The fuck kinda pussy drink is that shit?" erupted a man two stools beyond Frankie.

"You look as if you've already had a hard day, pal," Klinger told the interloper. "Me, I'm just getting up."

"How about you, buddy?" the bartender said, as he poured coffee into a white ceramic diner cup. "Same?"

"I'll have a stinger," Frankie said deliberately, as if addressing their bellicose neighbor.

"Okay," the bartender said smoothly, as he backed up Klinger's coffee with six cubes of sugar, a quart carton of cream, and four ounces of Jameson. "And how do you like your stingers?"

"Brandy from the well."

"Yeah?"

"White crème de menthe."

"Yeah."

"Maybe five to one."

"Gotcha . . ."

"Ice."

"Sure."

Frankie waited.

The bartender waited.

"That's it," Frankie said.

"Yeah." The bartender turned and began to search among the bottles behind him. "Aha," he said after a moment. He set a bottle on the bar. "I only got the green shit."

"That'll do," Frankie told him.

"On the rocks," the bartender assumed.

Frankie nodded patiently. "That's the ice."

The bartender put it together, served it, went away.

"When you don't know what the fuck they're asking you for," Frankie observed, "always ask them how they would build it if they were in your shoes."

"Works like a charm," Klinger agreed.

"Especially in a shithole like this place," said the man two stools away. His eyes were barely open. "Stinger my ass."

"You gotta point," Frankie said, lighting a cigarette.

Klinger raised the double. "Health and money."

The bartender put an ashtray on the bar in front of them.

Frankie, blowing smoke at the ceiling, added, "And the time to enjoy them."

The whiskey tasted mighty fine, although Klinger noticed that it aggravated a certain tightness, one might even say a pain, in his duodenum.

The man who had thought to object to Frankie's taste in drink laid his arm on the bar and his head on his arm and went straight to sleep. A few stools beyond him, where the bar made a right angle and headed toward the toilets, despite a certain intervening gloom, Klinger could see that the vertex of the right angle was already strewn with glasses, an ashtray full of butts, and two or three eviscerated dollar bags of tortilla chips. Each of the two men standing there was showing the other his knife.

Frankie fished an L-shaped piece of wire out of his pocket and twirled the longer leg of the L between the thumb and first three fingers of the hand between himself and Klinger. "Need a score?" He displayed the wire between them and below the edge of bar, so only Klinger could see it.

"Sure," Klinger said, "but I'm no dipper."

"Leave the dipping to me." The wire disappeared, and Frankie gave his cigarette some attention. "But I been in school and I'm a little rusty. The other night—." He directed a plume of smoke at the ceiling. "Anyway, I could use a shill."

The two men at the far end of the bar called the bartender, who attached his hand to an open quart of tequila on his way down there.

"Since when don't you go it alone?"

Frankie drew an ashtray close enough to tap his cigarette on its rim. "Since my second strike."

The two guys standing at the far end of the bar clicked glasses, downed their shots, and slammed the empties onto the bar.

Klinger sipped a little coffee. Really, really awful coffee. Plus it was cold. Plus it immediately aggravated the twinge in the lower forecourt of his gut. He traded the coffee for the whiskey and cleansed his palette.

"That sounds like a good reason for you to be, say, delivering groceries to shut-ins."

Frankie affected to brighten. "Sign me up. I bet them shut-ins got all kinds of stuff laying around. Stuff they don't need anymore. Gold chains and jewelry, for example. Watches. Hundred-dollar bills. Sterling silver bedpans."

Klinger laughed. "They haven't been letting two-time losers have rings of keys to apartments all over the city since the dot-com times, Frankie, back when nobody could find good help."

"I was inside at the time," Frankie agreed, "but I hear stories. Unbelievable stories."

"In every case," Klinger assured him, "they were almost certainly true."

Now, at the far end of the bar, thumps were to be heard. One two three four, four three two one. Syncopated thumps.

Klinger leaned away from the bar so as to see beyond the snoring drunk.

"They said it was like the Wild West," Frankie continued. "They said there was gold lining the streets, just waiting to be picked up. They said it was every man for himself, no quarter asked or given."

"That's a damned accurate description of the dot-com times," Klinger said. "What the fuck are those guys doing?"

Frankie, who had made no sign of paying attention to the far end of the bar, said, "You know mumblety-peg?"

One two three four.

Klinger thought about it. "You throw a knife at a tree. If your knife sticks, the other guy has to do it with his knife."

Four three two one.

"When somebody misses, he loses a point. Like that?"

"Yeah," Frankie said lazily. "Another way you can play, two guys stand six feet apart, each with his feet close together. At attention, like. The guy who goes first, he throws a knife close to one or another foot of the other guy. Eight or ten inches away, say. If the knife sticks in the ground, the guy has to move his foot out to it. Then it's his turn. If his throw sticks in the ground, the first guy has to move his foot out to the knife. And so forth. The first guy to fall over loses."

Klinger almost didn't laugh. "That sounds about as useful as watching television."

"Inside," said Frankie, "I learned to hate television."

"So what's that got to do—."

"Them guys down there are running a variation on the theme," Frankie said. "First, they down a shot of tequila."

"I saw that."

"Then, they flip a coin."

"I missed that."

"Guy that loses spreads his hand flat on the bar, fingers wide as they can go, like this."

"Okay."

"Then he takes his knife and stabs the point outside the thumb, then between thumb and forefinger, forefinger and fuck-you finger, fuck-you finger and ring finger, ring finger and pinky, outside. Then he goes back."

Klinger watched Frankie stab the fuck-you finger of his right hand sequentially between the fingers of his left hand, spread on the bar, and back.

"One two three four five six," Frankie counted, "six five four three two one."

"Isn't that kind of hard on the bar?" Klinger said.

Frankie shrugged. "Depends on what kinda joint you're in."

"Guess so," Klinger said.

"If you don't stab yourself . . ." Frankie continued.

". . . The other guy takes a round," Klinger concluded.

"But first," Frankie cautioned, "you down another shot."

As he said this, the bartender passed them with a tray of shot glasses, each brimming with tequila, a salt shaker, an ashtray heaped with lime sections.

"Then you do another round," Frankie said.

"Until the inevitable," Klinger concluded.

"Yeah," Frankie said. "And there's a lot of variations."

"Like . . . ?"

Frankie shrugged. "Each round goes a little faster."

"That sounds subjective."

"Many's the argument," Frankie agreed. "A less subjective variation is, the first round you go once, you have your drink, and the second round you go twice."

From the far end of the bar, a knife point touched the bar sixteen times.

"They musta heard me," Frankie said.

"Let me guess," Klinger said.

Frankie extended his hand, palm up. "After the second round, you could do two shots."

"And so forth."

"*Voilà*," Frankie said.

"A little more interactive than television."

Frankie shrugged. "There you go."

"Whatever happened to canasta?" Klinger asked. "You ever play this knife game?"

"Are you kidding?" Frankie asked. "I'm an artist. My hands is all I got."

"Of course," Klinger said. "I forgot."

"Them guys down there," Frankie said, though he'd yet to turn around for a look at them, "they probably make their living with their brains."

Klinger smiled.

"We ain't come to my favorite variation," Frankie said sleepily.

"What's that?"

Frankie pointed at his hand. "Instead of stabbing the knife between the fingers of your own hand, you stab it between the fingers of the other guy's hand."

"That's a prescription for escalation," Klinger said, moving his drink away from Frankie.

Frankie nodded.

Somebody at the far end of the bar yelled "FUCK!"

"Fuck?" The guy with his head on the bar woke up. "Did somebody say fuck?"

"Fuck! Shit! Ow!" the other voice continued.

A hearty guffaw issued from a third party. "Your round, motherfucker!"

"Ow! shit!"

"Let's get out of here," Frankie said to Klinger. "Finish your drink."

"Shit, shit, shit . . ."

Frankie slid his stinger over the bar. "You finish it."

"You fuckin' crybaby," declared the third voice.

SIX

Klinger and Frankie Geeze exited the Hawse Hole, on Polk just below Geary, at 10:35 in the a.m.

"Son of a bitch," Frankie said. He donned a very dark pair of designer shades against the overcast and smoothed the pinstriped lapels of his suit jacket.

Klinger had noticed the quality of Frankie's suit. But aloud he observed, "That oughta keep the rain off your peepers."

"Say," Frankie said, "I gotta make a stop."

"Why am I not surprised?" Klinger said.

"You hungry?"

"You see a door lately that I don't fit through?"

"No," Frankie said frankly.

"Okay," Klinger said.

"I know just the place," Frankie said.

"You buying?"

"Dude," Frankie said. "A guy like me don't sweat the odd twenty-dollar bill."

Klinger regarded Frankie with incredulity. "You're taking us someplace where breakfast cost twenty dollars?"

Frankie regarded him back. "Did I say that?"

"Well, no. Not exactly. But if that's your intention, let me take you someplace where it costs ten and you can give me the difference."

"I can see I'm dealing with a fiduciary sharpie, here."

Klinger drew himself up to his full five foot eight. "Not for nothing do I live in a SRO hotel."

Frankie resumed walking. "Not for much, either, I'll wager."

Klinger deflated. "True."

"Nevertheless, I can see that I'm going to have to watch my step with you."

"Hey," Klinger said modestly, "it's not like you're on the yard."

Never one to be easily fazed, Frankie stopped again, looked at Klinger again, then resumed walking again. "I'll tell the world," he muttered, laughing. Abruptly he wheeled and said, "You read the *New York Times*?"

"Every day," Klinger lied.

"Here." Frankie handed Klinger a twenty and pointed at a doorway. "If you can fit through that door, get one. Keep the change."

The doorway was actually next to a pass-through into a newsstand, of the type increasingly rare, through which only merchandise and money need fit. Porn magazines, cigarettes, porn DVDs, gum, porn VHSs, and not a few newspapers including, voilà, the *New York Times*. Klinger made the purchase and pocketed $17.80. Which fattened the bankroll, he calculated happily, to $23.69. Thing is looking up. That's right: thing, singular. As in, I see that you're getting your duck in a row. As in, chins up.

Klinger figured it was at least half Frankie's paper. "Want to see?"

"See what?"

"The paper. The news. What's going on. Iraq and shit."

Frankie smiled and shook his head. "You are a fucking trip."

By way of laboring up and out of the Tenderloin, they mounted the southwestern flank of Nob Hill. There, at the intersection of Pine and Hyde, Frankie showed Klinger a corner café and told him it was a place that catered to hospital staff. He jerked a thumb over his shoulder toward the lobby of St. Francis Memorial, right across Hyde Street. "I gotta date." Frankie gestured vaguely, against the traffic on Pine Street, toward the crown of Nob Hill. "Up the hill." He patted Klinger's shoulder. "No matter what happens, keep the faith, I'll be back. Shortly thereafter, you will experience a payday."

"I'm not sure my system can handle the shock," Klinger said truthfully.

"You got plenty of dough for this place," Klinger assured him. "Enjoy your breakfast. And hey," he flicked his fingertips at the shoulder. "Enjoy your lunch, too."

Klinger frowned. "How much time we talking, here?"

"What," Frankie asked. "You in a rush?"

Klinger lifted a shoulder. "No, I . . ."

Frankie raised his hand and, like magic, a green taxi glided silently to the curb. "Gotta keep up appearances," Frankie winked.

Frankie ducked into the back seat of the taxi, closed the door, and the machine glided soundlessly away. Clean Air Vehicle, it said on the cab's trunk, and Gentleman's Club. A block back down Hyde at Bush, which is one-way going east, the taxi forged a left through a crosswalk full of wheelchairs and crutches and disappeared.

Breakfast and lunch on the same day, Klinger marveled, as he contemplated the front door of the café.

Two and a half hours later, Klinger was holding at arm's length the full-page ad for an unputdownable thriller on the back of the Arts section when Frankie slid into the booth opposite him.

"I was just wondering," Klinger said, as he refolded the section and dropped it onto the stack beside his perfectly polished plate, "how long it's been since I read two articles in a row on the subject of narrative ballet."

JIM NISBET

"Yeah . . ." Frankie managed to respond. Despite the word's containing no fricatives, in Frankie's mouth it sounded like slurry running down the chute behind a cement truck. His lower lip hung a bit slack, and he appeared even more relaxed than the last time Klinger had seen him.

Even though the *Times* had fired up aggressive West Coast coverage of late, Klinger had found no mention in it of a San Francisco convenience store clerk getting his head bashed in by ten pounds of frozen chicken. Either way, he saw no reason to mention it to Frankie.

"Everything come out okay up the hill?"

"Beautiful . . ."

A waitress appeared with a pot of coffee and asked Frankie if he wanted anything.

"I'm . . ." Frankie managed to say, "I'm good . . ."

She indicated Klinger's cup. Klinger shrugged. As she poured the refill she asked, "Ever heard of a poet called Jim Gustafson?"

Frankie didn't bother to answer that one, but she wasn't talking to Frankie.

"Can't say as I have," Klinger responded politely.

The waitress parked the knuckles of her spare hand on her hip. "The night he read the line to a thousand people in the Exploratorium, about sitting in Malvina's and drinking coffee till your hands shake like the wings on cheap jets?" She smiled and nodded. "I took him back to my place and fucked him till he puked."

This got even Frankie's attention. "*Yeah . . .*"

"Didn't take long," she added.

"I remember Malvina's," Klinger said. "Over there in North Beach. Next to Washington Square."

"Jim was talking about the old Malvina's," the waitress told him. "On Union at Grant. Before it moved to Washington Square."

SNITCH WORLD

"Is it still there?"

"Beats me," she said. "I live in Bernal Heights."

"What about the poet guy?"

"Deader than a letter to Santa," she said. "The sauce got him."

"Sorry to hear it."

"We had our fun." She gathered up Klinger's empty plate with her free hand. "Then I threw him out. Anything else?"

Frankie looked as if he were about to manage a shrug, but the gesture eluded him.

"I think that's it," Klinger told her. "Let's have a check."

"You got it."

Klinger watched her walk away.

"Yeah . . ." Frankie's eyes were barely open, and he smacked his lips once in a while, ever so slightly.

Klinger folded his hands on the Formica and waited. Not two minutes later, the check came. The total was $9.87, in return for which Klinger had more food in his belly than any day in recent memory. Plus, he'd been taking up real estate for two and a half hours. He laid a ten and two ones on the tray. "Keep it." Eleven dollars and sixty-nine cents entered the ruled ledger of his mind.

"Appreciate it," the waitress said. If she noticed that Klinger's table-mate was on the nod, she made not a sign. Instead, once more, she showed Klinger the coffee pot. Klinger lifted both hands off the laminate and made them flutter. The waitress smiled and went away with the coffee and twelve bucks.

After fiddling with his cup for a few minutes Klinger got bored watching his host convincingly imitate a man catching forty winks in Business First. Plus, Klinger's ass was getting sore from abusing the Naugahyde. Not to get uppity, for he was as simultaneously sated and warm as he'd

57

been in weeks, if not months. Finally, he asked Frankie how long he'd been out.

Frankie frowned slightly. "About two weeks," he said, not bothering to open his eyes.

Klinger kept his voice down. "How the hell did you get a habit going in two weeks?"

Frankie smiled vaguely. "Who said I ever lost it?"

Oh, Klinger reminded himself, of course.

"Besides," Frankie added, allowing the hint of a frown to flit across his brow, "do I look like I gotta habit?"

For the first time in weeks, Klinger laughed without rancor.

Frankie opened his eyes a little wider. "Lemme tell you something about a habit."

Klinger made no response. He was going to hear about it whether he wanted to or not.

"As a musician once told me," Frankie said, "any time you see a sixteenth note? Or a whole row of them? And you gotta habit?" Frankie sailed the flat of his hand over the table. "Every one of them sixteenth notes looks like a half note."

"A half note," Klinger repeated.

"And you," Frankie said, "got allllll day," he floated the hand back over the table, "to play every one of them just right."

"That's . . ." Klinger pursed his lips, "persuasive."

Even with the shades between them, Klinger could see Frankie's eyelids flutter. It reminded him of the reflection of the revolving blades of a ceiling fan on the surface of his drink just . . . Was that yesterday?

"But," Klinger said, "you're not a musician."

"But," Frankie said, raising an admonitory if languid forefinger, "I am an artist."

"Ah ha," Klinger said. "I'd forgotten."

"Pay attention," Frankie suggested. Once again his hand sailed over the Formica, toward the window and beyond where a dog, as Klinger now noticed, crouched to defecate on the sidewalk, as its mistress patiently watched.

"I regard the teeming boulevard . . ." Frankie stopped. After a moment he said, "Where was I?"

"The teeming boulevard," Klinger prompted him. "You are an artist."

Again Frankie sailed the hand over the Formica. ". . . To and fro march the marks . . ." Frankie smiled. "Each and every one a half note."

"And you got allllll day," Klinger smiled, "to play them just right."

"Not all of them. By no means all of them." Frankie redeployed the forefinger. "Just the one. The exact right one."

"You're an artist," Klinger had to agree.

Frankie did not dissemble.

Klinger sat back against his side of the booth and fingered his cup of coffee. If Frankie noticed a pause, awkward or otherwise, he manifested no sign. I'm sick of drinking coffee, Klinger thought to himself, that's for sure. He glanced up. The clock on the wall above the entry door told him it was one-fifteen. This clock, too, had Chinese numerals. What the hell's with the Chinese numerals? A notice posted beside the clock announced opening time at six a.m. and closing time at two p.m. A notice posted on the other side of the clock announced the San Francisco Minimum Wage as $9.79 per hour.

Klinger's eyes fell until they found the waitress, who was behind the sit-down counter making a fresh pot of coffee.

"I'll bet you're thirsty," Frankie announced, as if reading Klinger's mind.

"Yes," Klinger admitted. "I'm about as caffeinated as I can stand." He lay the flat of his palm on the lower-left corner of his stomach. Though masked by satiety, the twinge lurked. "It's time to take the edge off."

"Let's go," Frankie said, without betraying the impulse to act on his own suggestion.

Klinger got to his feet.

"We'll take a cab to North Beach," Frankie said, still not getting up, his eyes slits. "Get you something to drink."

"Talk about your perfectly executed half notes," Klinger said. "But it seems fair to mention that I'm just about tapped."

Frankie opened his hand over the Formica, and a twenty-dollar bill, folded twice, fell out of it. "Be my guest." Klinger marveled at the twenty. Frankie stood out of the booth. "Taxi and drinks, on me."

Klinger shook his head. "Two weeks?"

No comment accompanied Frankie's fey gesture.

Gaining the sidewalk, Frankie said, "Jesus Christ," and reached into the inner breast pocket of his jacket.

"You already got them on," Klinger told him.

Frankie touched the hinge of his sunglasses with the other hand. "Oh."

The dog was tied to the parking meter nearest the corner. Seeing Klinger, it stood up and wagged its tail. Klinger offered him the backs of his fingertips. The dog licked them with barely a sniff, redoubling the oscillations of its tail. Klinger ruffled its ears. "Somebody's glad to see me."

"A little doggie every day," its owner said, as she dropped a bag of waste into a trash can beyond the parking meter, "is all a body needs."

"Yeah," Klinger murmured, as a taxi magically pulled to the curb. With not so much as a backwards glance at the woman or her dog, Frankie opened the curbside door and slid across the back seat. "Broadway and Columbus," he told the cabbie. "C'mon, man," he said to the open door.

"What's his name?" Klinger asked the owner.

"Douglas Englebart, Jr.," she told him.

"The—." Klinger frowned. "Who?"

"He's named for Douglas Englebart."

The dog sat down and looked expectantly up at his mistress. "I don't—," Klinger began.

"Sure you do." The woman fed the dog a biscuit. "He invented the mouse."

"The mouse?" Klinger repeated stupidly.

Frankie was chuckling, but at or with what or whom, it would have been difficult to say.

The woman made a squeezing motion with her free hand. "Point and click? Englebart," she laughed, "can you point and click?" The dog wagged its tail.

"Englebart," Klinger told the dog. The dog looked at Klinger. "I'll see you later." The dog turned its head. "Won't I see you later?" The dog furrowed its brow and turned its head the other way.

"He's hip to the interrogative tone," the woman said, "but he has no idea what you're asking."

Klinger nodded thoughtfully.

"Let's go!" Frankie said.

SEVEN

"The problem with this app," said the voice in the phone, "is that its memory footprint imposes conflicts in cache. Period."

Phone clasped to his right ear, Phillip Wong twirled fettuccine onto the fork in his left hand, its tines held against the curvature of the spoon in his right hand. "You're blaming my app for an out-of-date hardware fault," he protested. "That shit flies on the dual core." He filled his mouth with *pasta puttanesca*.

In the audio background, Enrico Caruso was shedding a fugitive tear. "Phil Phil Phil," the phone chided. "Do you have any idea of the ratio of dual-core owners versus every other goddamn phone on the market?"

"That's not my problem, Marci." Phillip dropped the spoon, took the phone to hand and glanced at the screen. At that moment, for some reason, he recalled a hod carrier he'd noticed on a construction site a couple of weeks back, stacking cinderblocks with a phone clenched between ear and shoulder. They'll have to build a special coffin for that guy, Phillip had thought at the time, with a dogleg toward the top. If I couldn't afford out-call shiatsu, I'd be courting a similar fate. He reparked the phone on his opposite shoulder and took up the fork. "Besides, it's nine fucking thirty. Can't this wait till tomorrow?"

"In two and a half hours, Phillip," Marci pointed out, "it will be tomorrow."

"Fuck, Marci," Phillip whined, "this is the first hot meal

I've had in, in . . ." He couldn't remember the last time he'd had a hot meal. He inserted a figure anyway. ". . . Two weeks."

"Show me where it says you are allowed hot meals," Marci said.

Phillip failed to dignify this quip with a laugh or an answer.

"More to the point," Marci continued, "does your hot-ass phone have a debugger and a compiler?"

Phillip dropped the fork, downed the second half of his Sangiovese, and waved the empty glass at the wait-staff. "No," Phillip told the phone, "but it did steer me to an empty table in a North Beach Italian restaurant on a Thursday night."

"That's a good app," Marci pointed out. "Too bad you didn't write it."

Not for nothing, Phillip cursed to himself, did some-body make this chick Vice President of Compliance. "True," he managed to retort despite a mouthful of pasta. "I use it every time I'm allowed to eat off-site."

His phone groaned. "What's that?"

"I just sent you a pdf of a monograph on software archi-tectures for real-time caching—nonconflicting real-time caching. It's a little theoretical and there's some math, but you can probably apply its wisdom to a patch for your code in time for a demo on Sunday morning."

"Sunday morning?" Phillip nearly screamed. The waiter appeared with the bottle and poured Phillip's glass half full. Phillip gestured. The waiter frowned. Phillip ges-tured again. Without missing a beat, the waiter retrieved a second glass from a setup on the adjacent table, filled that one half full, inclined his head slightly, and went away. Phillip downed half the first half-glass. "Sunday morn-ing . . ." he repeated, a little more calmly.

"It took all the persuasion this girl could muster to get

them to bump it from Saturday night. I bought you twelve hours."

"Twelve hours," Phillip repeated numbly.

"Aren't you going to thank me?"

"I'm . . ." Phillip toasted the air in front of him. "Pulverized with gratitude."

"Mere gratitude will get you nowhere," Marci pounced. "What I need is results. What I need is code that doesn't crash. What I need is the Phillip I went to college with, the Phillip who was too shy to sleep with me, the Phillip who wrote the code that caused our class robot to chain-saw MIT's robot in half and, when the contest committee disassembled our code, the first thing they discovered was seventeen bytes in the credit header that spelled out *I* ♥ *Marci Kessler*, including the extravagant three spaces, and the second thing they found out was that there wasn't an unoriginal thought in the whole twenty-five thousand instructions."

"But Marci," Phillip protested, "that was a robot. This is a fucking secondary app for a lonely hearts site designed to filter out date-rape potential."

"*So?*"

Phillip downed the second half of the first half-glass, set the empty down on the table next to him, and picked up the second half-glass. "So robots are not people," he pointed out.

"What's that got to do with anything?" Marci screamed.

If they'd been video-conferencing, Marci could have seen Phillip shrug as he switched the phone to his other ear and downed the first half of the second half-glass of wine. "What it's got to do with, Marci," he said as he lowered the glass, "is cache. People algorithms need bigger caches than robot algorithms." He burped. "It's—excuse me—that simple."

He could hear Marci taking a deep breath. "Phillip," she finally said. "How much is Corazonics paying you?"

"You know damn well how much you're paying me," Phillip told the phone. "To the penny."

"That's right, Phillip. To the penny. But I want to hear it from you."

"A hundred and twenty-five dollars an hour," Phillip said wearily. And it used to be worth it, he annotated to himself.

"That's right," Marci told him. "How often do you bill?"

"Every two weeks."

"And the last invoice?"

"Well I'm glad you brought that up, Marci," Phillip said, assuming the role of aggressor. He took a look at the screen of his phone and paged past the newly arrived pdf along with several recent text and voice messages until he'd accessed his cloud-based consultancy spreadsheet: "$18,375."

Despite her considerable crust, Marci gasped. "A tidy sum," she finally managed to point out.

"I earned every fucking cent of it," Phillip said evenly. "Do you know how much of my life that bill represents?"

"I'm sure it's on the invoice," Marci hedged.

"One hundred and forty-seven hours," Phillip told her. "Two seven-day weeks of ten-and-a-half-hour days. And just in case forty thousand lines of C-plus-plus don't verify that I was at least near the job if not on it, your brand-new and totally insulting electronic pass-key system will. I was on the job and on the case—compiling, debugging, running . . . On fumes, I might add, though I would stipulate they were high-octane fumes. As a matter of fact, Marci, I've been noticing something lately."

"Don't change the subject," Marci said quickly. A little too quickly.

"Well, Marci," Phillip said calmly, "I'm not changing the subject. Not really."

"Phillip . . ."

"When we got into this deal," Phillip interrupted, "I was promised equity."

"And when there is some goddamn equity," Marci came back, "you'll be the first to know."

Phillip took a beat. He looked at his pasta. Without even tasting it, he knew it had gone as cold as the untouched salad. Cold as the heart on the other end of the phone. Too cold for nourishment. Now he said, as if offhandedly, "I been hearing about an IPO."

Marci said nothing.

"Marci?"

"Phillip?"

"Well?"

"Well what?"

"I-P-O."

"That'd be sweet," she hedged.

"Especially if we had something written down."

Silence.

"My bad, of course," Phillip said simply. "For not getting something in writing, I mean."

More silence.

"My badder," Phillip continued, still with the calm voice, "for trusting you."

Silence.

"Know how I found out about it?"

No response.

"It's written on the back of the door of the second stall in the 27th-floor men's restroom. That's how."

Silence.

"Talk about your sit-down blog."

Silence.

"Huh, Marci?"

Silence.

"What's the deal, here? You know and I know that pro-grammers don't come much better than me, and the ones that do, you can't afford. They're all contractually locked up—and the key to that lock is equity. As if you didn't know. So I ask myself, Self, what's with all this pressure? This deal sucks. All I do is work, my work's never sufficient or good enough, there's always more to do than any one single prog-rammer can do, and, for the last few months, it's always been about stupid modules that have little or nothing to do with our original mission statement, which is, get this app up and running and selling, take it public, cash out, and get on to the next thing. Am I right?"

After a long pause, Marci sighed and said, "That was the deal. It still is."

"How many partners are there again?"

"You know the answer to that as well as I do."

"You, Steve, Vikram, Bill, Mary P., Mary Y. Is that all of them?"

As if reluctantly, Marci filled in a blank with, "You forgot Steve's father."

"Ah yes. The seed money. I guess you're not going to shaft him." After a pause, Phillip repeated the statement as a question. "I guess you're not going to shaft Steve's father?"

More silence.

"Marci?" he said incredulously.

"Yes, Phillip?" came the chilly response.

Game over, Phillip said to himself. Phillip turned the stem of his wineglass between his fingers. The tablecloth beneath began to twist. One fucking year. He turned the stem the other way. The cloth untwisted. If only it were so simple. Times like these, he said to himself, it's best not to be drinking so much. He lifted the glass and downed half of it. Or not at all, he added, setting the glass back on the table. If you don't watch your own back, he reflected bitterly, nobody's going to watch it for you. Not even your own son.

Maybe especially not even your own son.

"Phillip . . ." Marci began tentatively.

Certainly not your longest acquaintance and best friend from technical college, the sharpest manager you'd thought you ever met, and good-looking, too—although what that latter qualification had to do with the equation, he'd long since forgotten. Why, after all, expect her to watch your back, when she's obviously been exclusively preoccupied for a long time with watching her own?

Phillip sighed heavily, and his entire frame sagged. He'd been harboring a lot of tension for a lot of time, and he knew it, even as he denied it. Though he'd seen this confrontation coming for a while, he'd refused to allow himself to believe its subject. Marci Marci Marci. Sold out, copped out, and with a little help from the fiancé, whom Phillip had always pegged as venal, dishonest, corruptible, clutching for the main chance—mere emotional or maybe human entanglements from the past be damned.

"I'm sorry, Phillip," Marci suddenly said.

He almost didn't hear it. "Sorry?" he repeated.

Marci said nothing.

"Are you going to pay that invoice?" he asked.

"I'll . . . see what I can do."

"It's not my fault it was bullshit work," Phillip reminded her. "Work tasked to me specifically to force me to quit." He took a beat. "Right?"

"You've no call to take that attitude," Marci said quickly. "It's not like we haven't already paid you—how much?"

"Well over three hundred thou," Phillip said immediately.

"Not bad for one year," she suggested.

"One year of my life," he agreed. "One year without even the time to pick up my dry-cleaning. Though I was looking at it as an investment."

"Well," she said, "what did you do with the money?"

Phillip pursed his lips. Less rent on his crummy apartment, and the occasional fleeting and very modest night out, like this one, he still had most of it. "That's none of your business, Marci. Not to mention, it's beside the point."

"What point?"

"You're shafting me. You know it, I know it, all the aforementioned shitheads know it and—what I consider worse?"

"What do you consider worse, Phillip?" Marci said, suddenly coming on with the acid tone. "Darfur? Bangladesh?"

"What's worse," Phillip said, declining to take the bait, "is that if I knew it I suppressed it, and if I suppressed it it's because I trusted you and your shitbird husband-to-be."

"Let's leave Billy out of this."

"Leave Bill out this? Gladly. Only it's not possible. Or—hey, maybe it is possible. One thing would make it possible. One thing."

"What thing is that?"

He was testing her attention span. He could hear the strain. She was probably already browsing the latest posts to her bridal registry. The conversation was almost over. All he had to do was quit and they could hang up and everybody could get on to the next multiplicity of tasks.

"That thing would be this: that you set me up for this from the beginning. You recruited me into the start-up, there was a promise of equity, it was a promise that you never intended to fulfill. True or false? If true, well, sure: I'll gladly leave Bill out of it."

"What are you saying, Phillip?" There was nothing but ice in her voice now, arctic ice, many feet deep.

"I'm saying...I'm saying..." Phillip stared at the inch of Sangiovese that remained in the second glass, which was actually his third glass. It would have been nice to throw it across the room. A mere gesture, but nice. Ditto, it would have perhaps been satisfying to turn over the table. It may even have been conciliatory to duke it out with the staff. But there was no percentage there. No equity...They just ran a modest little cucina Italiana, and they ran it well. The food was good. The wine was reasonably priced. It wasn't their fault that Phillip was in bed with the wrong people in some other business in some other location. No. That was Phillip's fault, and Phillip's fault only. Phillip had only the one person to blame, himself to blame, and it was a lesson that perhaps most people who had managed to achieve the ripe old age of twenty-six had already learned but had somehow eluded him.

Until tonight.

"I quit," Phillip told his phone.

"Submit that in writing," Marci said quickly. "Word the document as a respectful resignation, along with a quit-claim, and send me the pdf. Include with it a copy of your final invoice marked net five and say as much. I'll see that you're paid in full within sixty days, and we'll give you our highest recommendation."

Before Phillip could point out that net five means five business days, not thirty or sixty, she rang off.

He rested his phone hand on the red and white checked table cloth. The phone was hot and so was his right ear. Both were hotter than his meal.

He stared at the nearly full bowl of pasta puttanesca in front of him.

He tugged the red and white checked napkin away from his shirt collar, dabbed his lips *pro forma*, and laid it neatly atop his salad fork.

One year, he was thinking, if he was thinking anything at all. But he'd known Marci since Computer Club in high school, which made ten years, or thirty-eight percent of his life, and that seemed a treachery no amount of cognition could rectify.

An odd noise from the phone let Phillip know that its battery was low.

Phillip drew his attention to the phone. On its screen various widgets blinked, spun, floated, came and went. Of the five of them Phillip had written single-handedly, Corazonics controlled three.

Let it die.

He dropped the phone in his breast pocket.

After paying the bill, Phillip wandered north on Kearny to the intersection at Columbus. There, at Café Niebaum-Coppola, he sat still long enough to purchase and consume a shot of Haitian rum with an espresso. But the place was too brightly lit, and the movie posters and the crowd they attracted did nothing for him. He crossed Kearny and then Washington and stepped into Mr. Bings, where he ordered a rum and coke. Before long he abandoned the drink and a ten-dollar bill on the bar because the European football game on the big screen only aggregated to the perceived sumtotal of meaninglessness. From there he drifted up the block to Vesuvio, where he lingered over another rum and coke long enough to watch a chess game. But it turned out the two players were recreating a game Samuel Beckett designed to be played in the madhouse toward the end of *Murphy*, which Phillip only divined because one of the players was calling out the moves from a copy of the novel. In the first half of the game, the pieces tentatively advance toward one another. In the second half, they retreat. What's the point?

He wandered up the avenue. He crossed Broadway,

JIM NISBET

took a left on Vallejo, a right on Powell. At the far end of
the block, where Powell comes back to Columbus, he hit
an ATM for two hundred dollars, around which he folded
the dwindling remains of the previous two hundred dollars, inserting the resulting sheaf of bills into the right
front pocket of his jeans, beneath the skirt of the tweed
jacket he'd bought at Barney's, in New York, the year they'd
won the battle of the robots. It was the only tweed jacket he
owned, and it had leather patches on its elbows.

A block away, at Gino & Carlo, on Green Street, Phillip
switched to margaritas. Miles Davis was on the jukebox.
The bar was crowded, convivial, boisterous. Phillip almost
felt at home. He ordered a second margarita. It tasted good,
it made him feel better, it made no difference that the room
was spinning. A solid year of stress began to shed down his
shoulders like rain off a dog, therefrom to flood across the
barroom floor and dissipate through the cracks into who
knew how deep a karmic basement, not like rats leaving a
sinking ship, he smiled to think, but like parasites desert-
ing a host they'd bled dry. This feels great, Phillip said to
himself. He even repeated it out loud, apropos of nothing,
to a guy sitting next to him. You got that right, said the guy
to Phillip, barely audible though other people's yelling, and
they touched glasses.

Not long after that Phillip had the idea of going down
to Enrico's, where he hadn't been in a long time, because
they served food there very late, and he had a vague idea
it was good food and, after that misfired Italian meal, he
found himself hungry enough to try again. For sure he
remembered the custom mix of local olives served in oil
from the Napa Valley with fresh-baked bread he could
order there, not to mention a good glass of wine, and, mut-
tering an adios to his stool mate, Phillip sallied into the
night.

Across Green Street, two men lounged in the doorway of a darkened store specializing in used vinyl, used stereo equipment, and used musical instruments.

"Here he comes," one said to the other.

EIGHT

An hour and a half later the mark came out of the Chat Noir on the south side of Broadway, directly across the street from Enrico's. He faced east, paused, faced west, paused, then exhaled loudly.

The sidewalk was teeming, the neon was screaming.

Whoooee, Phillip Wong was thinking. I may be six foot three, but those two Rusty Nails got me nailed to a tree.

The rhyme caught his fancy, and he began to repeat it under his breath. Six foot three, nailed to a tree. Six foot three...

Klinger, moving east, went port-to-port with the mark, nudging the left shoulder with his own left shoulder. "Oh, excuse me, buddy," Klinger said, turning to his right. The mark, who had been turned maybe forty-five degrees, barely noticed. "No problem," he said, just as Frankie Geeze went starboard to starboard with him.

"Oh, hey, hey, watch where you're goin'," Frankie said cheerfully. He took a step forward as he spoke, then turned a quarter turn back. "You okay, fella?"

Phillip Wong turned to his right and, being as he was about fifteen minutes from taking a nap in the gutter, straightened up, smoothed the front of his jacket and, marshaling all the dignity he had left, had a look at both of his fellow pedestrians and said, "I'm just fine, thank you. Dandy all 'round. No problem. No problem. Six foot three." He cleared his throat. "Always a silver lining," he said thoughtfully. The prospect of eight or ten hours' sleep, uninterrupted by cache overflows and rude phone calls, looked pretty good to him.

"Glad to hear it."

"Me, too, fella," Klinger said, moving east. "Have a swell night."

"Say," Frankie Geeze said, as Phillip Wong turned to his left to watch Klinger fade toward the intersection at Kearny, "can you tell me where the Ferry Building is?"

Phillip Wong turned back to his right. "The Ferry Building?" He frowned. "The Ferry Building . . ."

"That's okay," Frankie told him. "I'll find the mother-fucker. You—."

Phillip pointed west, toward the Broadway Tunnel, then lifted his hand, still pointing, over Frankie's head, and swung it back down Broadway until it was pointed east. Then, turning with the hand, he pointed more or less southeast. "Down to the bottom of Broadway, across the Embarcadero, take a right. You'll be on the water. Right away, you come to Pier 7. Can't miss it. It's a so-called fishing pier, though there's no more fish, and it's all lit up. Like me." Phillip chuckled. He converted the more or less horizontal pointing finger into the vertical one of pedagogy. "North of the Ferry Building," he informed Frankie, who listened patiently, "the piers are all odd-numbered. South of the Ferry Building . . ." Phillip's voice trailed off.

"They're even," Frankie helpfully supplied.

"That's it," Phillip said, staggering a little. "Too late for more ferries, though," he lamented.

"That's okay," Frankie said. "I'm supposed to meet a chick in a bar down there. How far is that?" Frankie shot a pinstriped cuff and had a look at a nice watch whose face lay on the inside of his wrist. "Damn."

Phillip screwed up his face. "That's gotta be half a mile." He pulled forward the left lapel of his British tweed jacket with his left hand and reached for the inside pocket with his right. "I could ask my phone—."

"Not to worry, pal," Frankie said mildly, touching the mark's wrist. "I got half an hour."

"Oh," Philip said, dropping the lapel. "You'll make the date. Easy."

"Yeah," Frankie told him. "Time to enjoy the full moon."

Phillip turned east again. There, not a hand's breadth above Berkeley, hung a huge moon, full and very orange.

"It must have just risen," Phillip marveled. "Wow."

"If it's setting over there," Frankie suggested, "we're in a world of shit."

For the second time in less than a minute, Phillip managed a chuckle.

"Gotta go," Frankie told him, and he went.

Phillip, watching the moon, nodded distantly.

Two-thirds of the Broadway block beyond Kearny, Frankie passed Klinger, who was ambling along with his hands in his pockets, and took a right at Montgomery. A couple of minutes later, just below the entrance to the parking lot at Verdi Place, Klinger caught up with him. "So?"

Frankie showed a thickness of freshly laundered twenties, folded once across the middle.

"A horizontal jeans pocket, and under the hem of a jacket too," Klinger marveled. "A clean piece of work."

"I was afraid I'd lost my touch inna joint," Frankie said simply.

"No way," Klinger assured him. "If I had a GED certificate, I'd sign it over to ya."

"But to tell you the truth," Frankie continued modestly, "that guy gave me so much time I coulda took his shorts off him. He never woulda noticed the difference." Frankie opened the folded bills and slid the thickness of the stack between thumb and forefinger. "Take," he said, giving, and "Count," he added, without bothering to do so himself.

Despite the dim light Klinger counted five twenties, a ten, four ones, and said as much. "One fourteen."

"Fifty-fifty." Frankie slipped his half of the take into the breast pocket of his jacket and patted it. Then he patted the breast pocket into which Klinger had deposited his own cut. "Thanks. And now we part ways."

Klinger frowned. "That enough for you?"

"Sure." Frankie smiled. "Who needs to eat?"

The roar crescendoed into a howl more to be expected from a man desperate to wake from a bad dream than from a mere victim whose pocket has been picked. Before either felon could react, Phillip plowed into them from behind, launching Frankie headlong down the steepness of Montgomery. As Phillip ricocheted into Klinger, he tackled him at the waist.

Klinger, though a slacker when it came to physical altercation, did what he thought he had to do, which was bring both fists, one clasped inside the other, down onto the back of Phillip's neck. To little discernible effect. On the contrary, having hurtled down the hill, aided and accelerated by gravity, Phillip's forward momentum, though shared with Frankie, pinballed the two of them across the breadth of the sidewalk.

A peculiarity of this sidewalk is that it forms the eastern border of a two-level parking garage. The top level is accessed from Broadway. Access to the lower floor, ten feet below the upper, is made via Verdi Place, off Montgomery Street.

The upper deck, of poured pre-stressed concrete, being more or less flush with the elevation of Broadway, flies south over the Verdi entrance until it's a full story and a half higher than Montgomery Street. The upper deck is supported by a fourteen-inch grade beam. Between the apex of this beam, where it meets the pavement of Verdi, and the end of the parking lot, perhaps five car-widths south, a long, right-angle triangle opens up. Its upper leg is level, and it extends from the apex at Verdi to the northernmost exterior wall of the next building south. This wall forms a right angle with the upper car deck, and descends about eight feet to the incline of the Montgomery sidewalk. This sidewalk, if you walk back up the hill, north, forms the hypotenuse of the right triangle, tapering through the angle back to the foundation of the Verdi pavement.

This entire triangle is open. Once upon a time, perhaps, there had been fencing over this cavity, or pigeon netting, or a handrail. But no longer.

It was through this opening that Phillip Wong's forward moment carried Klinger, despite Klinger's frantic, if momentary, resistance. But, in fact, if Klinger had been able to foresee the end result, he might have resisted not at all. Precipitated backward, Klinger also twisted and fell to his right, down the hill, and, as he was shot almost horizontally through the aperture, like a perfectly cued eight ball, not so much as grazing above or below, the upper deck's grade beam peeled Phillip Wong off Klinger's hip as if he were a spud and his aggressor its epidermis, fracturing the skull of the victim—for Phillip Wong remains the victim in this, does he not?—though not killing him outright, and depriving him of his consciousness.

Klinger, for his part, fell several feet onto the hood of a brand new Jaguar XKR, indenting the cobalt blue sheet metal considerably, rolled half over and fell again, to the concrete between cars. The former impact sent a formidable boom reverberating among the parked vehicles, whose echoes eclipsed the grunt evinced by the latter.

This isn't working out, Klinger said to himself, as he

rolled over onto his back, but you got to get up anyway. He clawed at the Jaguar tire in the darkness. You got to get up! How come this car's alarm didn't go off? Get up . . .

Squinting in the dark, he heard a groan.

"Frankie," he whispered.

Klinger pulled himself up by the Jaguar's bumper, then by its eponymous hood ornament. The lower ledge of the opening was too high for him to see over. He moved south along the angle of the sidewalk until he could see over it. There, across the sidewalk and face down in a treebox, he could discern the crumbled outline of his erstwhile partner, Frankie Geeze.

Frankie looked a lot like a pile of laundry.

Klinger stuck his head out, over the hypotenuse of the sidewalk, and looked up the hill. There he discerned another pile of laundry, and from it the groan repeated.

Though this was North Beach, the street was dark and there seemed to be nobody around. "Frankie," Klinger hissed. He got one foot onto the front bumper of a Jeep Cherokee and levered a third of himself through the angled opening. "Frankie!"

Scrabbling for a purchase by which to lever himself through the hole, Klinger's uphill hand, his left, came wet away from the sidewalk. This gave him pause. By the miserable illumination available, his hand glistened black. He looked left. A gleaming trail led up the hill to the second pile of laundry.

Somebody dies in the commission of a felony, no matter how, it's called aggravating circumstances. It doesn't matter who dies, either. It could be a victim, it could be a bystander, it could be a perpetrator, it doesn't matter. The devil-djinn of gotcha squirm snapped one talon off the pastern of another: an accomplice gets the death house.

Klinger sagged against the concrete. Shit, he said to

himself. What started out as a bit of wage-earning has become gravid with seriousness.

And before he could assemble a more coherent synapse, blue and red lights and two or three registers of sirens converged on both ends of the block.

Both feet on the front bumper of the Jeep, Klinger reversed himself into a crouch so that now his back was against the outside wall of the parking garage, with his head below the angle of the sidewalk above.

Frankie's got a lot to lose with this one, Klinger told himself, but the one thing he won't do is dime me. Still . . . He reversed himself again and stuck his head up sufficient to catch a glimpse of the closer pile of laundry, just across the sidewalk. "Frankie," he hissed. "Get up!"

Headlights swiveled through the upper branches of the tree against whose trunk Frankie lay crumpled, as a fire truck turned south off Broadway and down Montgomery, not 150 feet up the hill. "Frankie," Klinger implored. "Make a move!"

No response. The headlights clambered down through the tree, through branches, forks and twigs, until the trunk glowed like a milepost. Klinger lowered his head until just his eyes and the dome of his forehead showed over the pavement. The siren decrescendoed and lowered in pitch. The first truck arrived with a hiss of airbrakes. Klinger ducked.

Doors opened and closed and a radio crackled. In the dark below the opening, now randomly traversed by red and white lights, Klinger made a snap decision. He let his feet drop from the Jeep bumper, duck-walked between it and the sidewalk until the wall was higher than his five foot six, then darted between the Jaguar and the last vehicle north.

As he made his way across the garage he heard a second truck arrive, from the south, followed by an ambulance. Not far away the distinct siren of a police car lifted into the night. No surprise there; it's a mere four and a half blocks to central station at Vallejo and Stockton. Then a second siren. And, further away, a third. The intersection of Montgomery and Broadway was turning into a big deal.

He passed a pickup truck whose bed was heaped with trash. He plucked a scrap of dark fabric from it, wiped the blood off the side of his left hand, and buried the rag under a thickness of lawn trimmings.

On the west side of the lower garage, a ramp inclined up to the Broadway level. Klinger took it, smoothing his clothes and hair as he went. Once on top, he wove a path through the thickly parked vehicles until he achieved the attendant's shack, hard by the street exit. A guy seated on a stool, in darkness illuminated by a small television, looked at him.

"Hey, buddy," Klinger said, "you seen the guy drives that Jag roadster, parked on the lower deck?"

"No," the attendant said, not looking up from his screen. "What about him?"

"He must still be in the bar," Klinger said.

"He's always in the bar," the attendant said. "He owns the fucking bar."

"That's why I like to hang out with him," Klinger said. "As opposed to you."

The attendant maintained his attention on his television with barely a grunt.

"They gotta be fake," a man on the screen said to a woman.

"Nope," she responded proudly, "though it's nothing you're ever going to find out for yourself."

Canned laughter followed Klinger to the Broadway sidewalk. He merged and headed west with some dozen others, weaving among additional dozens walking the other way. Fifty yards behind him the after end of a ladder truck, most of its length hidden by the building on the corner at Montgomery, blocked one of the two eastbound lanes of Broadway. At Kearny Klinger crossed Broadway with the light and walked straight up the hill. A breeze had sprung up at his back, from the southwest, and it helped. When he'd labored all the way up the carless block, which is close to a forty-degree grade, too steep for cars, he took the staircase to Vallejo, and continued past Green Street. At Union Street he took a left, and half a block later he took another left into an alley called Varennes Street. Varennes brought him back to Green, at which he took a left and, ten feet later, another left, into the front door of Gino & Carlo, where, despite a double thickness of people crowding the bar, he was able to get his hands around a double shot of Jameson on the rocks within two minutes. Its taste barely overcame the bitterness of the epinephrine that had zincked his palate.

NINE

He set the empty glass on the bar and moved to the door. The blustery southwest harbinger that had followed him up the Kearny steps was now making good on its promise of rain. Klinger turned up his collar, forged his way through the smokers huddled in the entry, and stepped onto the sidewalk.

At Stockton he took a left and hustled south, wind and rain in his teeth. Excepting staff who surrounded big tables in the backs of darkened restaurants, the storefronts of Chinatown were shuttered. For no reason at all, Klinger remembered that 94133 is Chinatown's ZIP code.

To forestall an inevitable soaking and in the hope that the rain would let up, he lingered at the southern mouth of the Stockton Tunnel until a passing southbound articulated bus—three axles, the latter two bearing two sets of double wheels each—drenched him good and proper. So much for that snap decision. He debouched into the downpour and slogged the remaining eleven blocks to the Hawse Hole.

Habit dies hard. It never once occurred to Klinger to take a bus. Or to try another bar. Or to mug a pedestrian for an umbrella.

The bar was still open. Klinger asked to borrow a towel. The bartender tossed him one that, though already damp, was a lot drier than Klinger. He mopped his face, draped the towel over a stool, sat on it, and ordered a mug of hot water with sugar, lemon, and a double-shot of Jameson.

"Oho," the bartender said, setting to work on the drink. "The ship came in, did it?"

Klinger bethought the dignity of his low profile. "The pneumonia has me dreaming of better times. Make that whiskey from the well. All else the same. After all," he added, "what can you charge a man for hot water?"

"Four dollars and fifty cents," the bartender readily admitted. "And it's still cheaper than health insurance."

"Point taken." It tasted like health insurance, too. Before five minutes had elapsed, Klinger ordered another.

Down by the bend in the bar, two guys were playing finger finger whosegottafinger. One two three four, four three two one. Shot glasses and knife blades gleamed in the gloom.

The bartender finished topping off six thimbles of tequila and delivered them to the bend in the bar on a tray. The thick bottoms of the shot glasses made short arcs in the gloom. The bartender returned to the cash register with an ashtray heaped with wrung-out wedges of lime and rang up forty-eight dollars. When the drawer sprang open he stuffed three twenties into the tray, extracted a ten and two ones, closed the drawer, and tucked the tip into a stein next to the register.

One two three four, four three two one.

One hundred and fourteen dollars plus eleven sixty-nine equals $125.69, Klinger was thinking. Less the nine bucks I just spent here, plus a dollar tip makes ten, leaves one sixteen, less the twelve plus three-dollar tip for the double Jameson in North Beach, leaves the cruising kitty with one-oh-oh sixty-nine. A long day's work, but not bad. Unless you count Frankie Geeze coldcocked on the sidewalk not five feet from an equally cold-cocked mark, and how is that one going to play out?

Klinger turned the steaming mug between the fingers

of both hands as he considered this. If the mark were alive, Frankie was in a tough spot. If the mark was dead, maybe Frankie could claim he got creamed trying to come to the mark's aid when he was getting mugged. This might fly until the cops pulled Frankie's jacket, which would take about five minutes, after which things would go tough for Frankie.

One two three four, four three two one.

That was stupid, a minute ago, letting this guy behind the plank think I was holding more pelf than usual, Klinger told himself. If I'm going to persevere with the life of crime, I gotta start keeping track of that kinda shit. It's one thing to spring for a double shot of top shelf booze in a crowded joint where everybody's drunk and nobody knows you. It's another to be throwing money around where you're a regular who's known for being regularly broke. It smacks of a big score. Word gets around. Next thing you know . . .

Big score. Listen to you. A hundred bucks and a major snafu to boot. Come to do the books, two major snafus and only a hundred bucks to show for it. It's a wonder I'm not dead or in jail or both. But, really, Klinger had no room to complain. When the sun rose on him two days ago, he had nothing.

Or had that particular sun risen just yesterday?

Klinger thought about it. He'd spent last night in the hotel upstairs. The night before, he'd slept in a bed of Mexican sage in Buena Vista Park. Mary Fiducione had stood him to a hot bath and a meal and a C-note. So it had been just since yesterday morning that he'd . . . That he'd what?

Klinger ordered a third drink.

Now it's down to $87.19.

So he had two nights left on his hotel: wait. He glanced at the Chinese clock on the wall above the cash register. Twelve-thirty. The bar clock would be fifteen minutes fast but, still, he had what was left of tonight and tomorrow night in the hotel. The smart thing to do would be to get a bottle, if drinking himself to sleep was what he was planning on doing, and pay in advance for three or four more nights in the hotel, which would still leave him a couple of bucks to eat on. Put it on the come, as his daddy used to say. Which was just about all Klinger could remember about his daddy.

A guy came in the bar, had a look around, and made as if he thought the stool next to the game of mumblety-finger was an obvious perch at which to make himself comfortable. The guy nodded at the bartender, the bartender spun a coaster onto the bar in front of him. They exchanged words. The bartender came back up the bar, set up two shot glasses with a rocks glass and said to Klinger, "You got a friend in the booze business." He moved his head toward the bend in the bar. "Still fancy the Jameson?"

Klinger glanced sideways down the bar, but his benefactor was absorbed in the game and ignored him. "Don't mind if I do."

"Same setup?"

Klinger nodded. The bartender added a coffee mug to his lineup and went about his business. Klinger went back to inhaling the fumes coming off his remaining grog, holding the mug to his nose with both hands, staring at the back bar, suppressing the occasional full-frame shiver. The future receded to a tantalizing distance of two, maybe three days, among the bottles and beer advertisements beyond the cash register, below the Chinese clock, within the frame of a well-begrimed proscenium, hand-carved in the nineteenth century—whereat the scenario dwindled to the last pixel dead center in the depowered cathode ray tube of his prescience.

Four two three one, one two "Ow! Fuck!" came the shout from the other end of the bar. "Fuck fuck fuck!" One of the players hopped through a circle with one hand in his mouth while the other player and their new friend laughed at him.

The bartender set a fresh mug of grog and the double shot of Jameson on fresh coasters in front of Klinger and took the other drinks down to the far end of the bar.

Everybody raised their glasses or mug toward one another, then quaffed. For the two mumblety-peg players it was top-shelf tequila as usual, and bottoms up.

The bartender came back up the duckboards, rang up the sale, put a couple of twenties into the register, retrieved a five and a couple of quarters, and added them to the tip jar.

Somebody's making a living, Klinger observed to himself. He inhaled the fumes off his fresh mug of grog. They smacked of quality.

And Klinger? Klinger was in the position nine-tenths of humanity finds itself in, which is, if you're not spending money, nobody returns your calls.

Such is the little bifurcation as I'm allowed, Klinger was thinking to himself, one or two bifurcations later, from the path of righteousness, onto the path of a little greater righteousness. I don't even have a driver's license anymore. Why should I be held to account? If you come to a fork in the road, Yogi Berra is reputed to have said, take it. But as Klinger saw the scenario, if you come to a fork in the road, take it to a pawnshop. Good whiskey or bad, if I don't get out of these clothes soon, I—.

"Hey," the bartender said again. "You in there?"

Klinger, recollecting himself to the present, blinked. The mug was still poised in front of his face, the balance of its contents warming him from within. The Chinese clock told him it was five minutes after one in the morning.

"I'm here," Klinger declared. "Where else would I be?"

The bartender nodded. "Guy who's been buying your drinks?"

Klinger waited.

"He'd like a word."

Klinger slid his eyes down the bar. Game in abeyance, the two mumblety-peg players leaned on the bar, talking. The third guy had his back to Klinger.

"Sure," Klinger said. "About what?"

The bartender smiled. "I have no idea." And he set about loading spent shot glasses into the little under-counter washing machine.

Klinger roused himself to call down the bar. "Hey." The three men looked his way. "Thanks." Klinger raised his drink. "What's up?"

The guy seated on the stool gestured.

Klinger took his drink down there.

The guy was bigger than he had looked from the other end of the bar. So were his friends.

"Klinger," he said to the guy who might be thought of as generous.

"Tommy," the guy said. Tommy and Klinger shook hands, each clasping the other's hand as if it were the handle on a stein of beer. The mumblety-peg players weren't introduced.

"I gotta piss," one of them abruptly said. "Me too," agreed the other. They made themselves scarce.

Klinger watched them go.

"You're friend a Frankie Geeze," Tommy said.

Klinger didn't freeze, exactly, but he assumed a mantle of caution. "That's true," he allowed. "Spent a little time with Frankie just this morning," he added, "as it happens. We had breakfast."

"I seen ya," Tommy said. "That's why I asked Bruce, there," he indicated the bartender, "to speak to ya. I got a little job. Real little." Tommy squinted. "You need a little job?"

"Depends," Klinger lied by way of hedging. "I like little. Big stresses me out."

"Yeah," Tommy smiled. "Stress sucks."

Klinger managed a smile, too. "How little?"

Tommy shrugged. "Little cab ride, little delivery, another cab ride, a little payoff. Like that."

Klinger nodded.

"I'm fronting cab fare." Tommy produced a wad sufficiently fat that extracting its thickness from the side pocket of his leather jacket gave him an awkward moment. He peeled three twenties off it, laid them on the bar, and, not far away, he laid down a hundred-dollar bill. "When you get back, the C-note is yours."

Klinger glanced toward the clock. "It's—."

"Not to worry," Tommy told him. "The light'll be off but the door will be open. Just knock." He rapped the knuckles of the wad-burdened fist on the bar, one-two, one-two, one. "Bruce likes to have a couple of belts after hours." He chucked Klinger lightly on the shoulder with the same knuckles. "He likes company, too."

"Occupational hazard," Klinger nodded.

"Wanna bump?" Tommy asked him.

Klinger shook his head. "I can't handle the crank," he said, "Shit burns too much."

"Who said anything about fuckin' crank?" Tommy spoke as if his feelings were hurt.

"Oh, well," Klinger said. "In that case . . ."

"Wait'll the fellas get back."

"And, what am I delivering?"

"Not a big deal," Tommy smiled. His teeth were narrow and yellow, their gums pink and receded. He pointed at Klinger's jacket. "It's already in your pocket."

"Hey," Klinger smiled weakly. "I guess you are a friend of Frankie's."

"Taught me everything I know and most of what I forgot," Tommy said. "I gotta lotta respect for Frankie."

Klinger nodded faintly. "Frankie's the best."

The two mumblety-peg players returned. At a sign from Tommy, each shook hands with Klinger. "'Sup," each of them said, "'sup." The second handshake left a flat bindle in the curled fingers of Klinger's right hand.

"Better take a piss before you head out," Tommy suggested. "There might be traffic or somethin'."

Klinger visited the men's room and snorted one line per nostril. When he came back he offered to shake hands with any of the three men standing there, so as to pass the bindle back, but they waved him off.

The bar telephone rang and Bruce answered it. "Somebody call a cab?" he asked the room.

"Cathedral Hill Apartments," Tommy told Klinger. "Opposite St. Mary's. Tell the doorman to ring Apartment 1426, then wait." He turned to the bar. "Brucie. Another round."

Klinger was in the cab and four blocks away when he realized that the substance in his maxillary sinuses was maybe only half cocaine, and the other half was probably heroin. He might have known. At least he assumed it was heroin. By the time the cab got to Geary and Van Ness, Klinger was pretty sure he was rhino-metabolizing speedball, and he was thrilled. Well well well, he marveled, as the taxi climbed the grade, a real vacation at last. It's been a long time since I've been cold and wet and not even able to feel it. Let alone, give a shit. He fingered the bindle in his pocket. I might not catch pneumonia after all.

The light at Gough was red. "Can't make a left," the cabbie said to the rear-view mirror. "Gotta go around." He made a circle with a forefinger. "Loop de loop."

"Yeah yeah," Klinger happily told him. "Whatever," he added; but what he was thinking was, "*mellow*."

The cabbie stood on the hydrogen, and his taxi

hummed downhill to Laguna, where he took a right to Post, another right uphill to Gough, another right back down to Geary, and finally diagonaled across the intersection and four lanes of no traffic into the circular drive in front of Cathedral Hill Apartments. Klinger told him to wait.

A doorman buzzed Klinger into the lobby and made a call. Five minutes later a little old lady exited an elevator and greeted him like her long lost nephew.

"My prescription," she enthused, and she traded the envelope Klinger pulled out of his jacket pocket for one of her own, which looked a lot like a package from a pharmacy, printed up one side and down the other with do's and don'ts. "Please give Dr. Flagon my new scrip, which I will require to be filled by this time tomorrow night at the very latest," she said with emphasis. "Be sure to remind him of that, and here's a little something for your trouble, you darling young man." She pressed a folded twenty into Klinger's hand. "It's so late for you to be working," she embellished, "and in the rain, too." She patted his arm. "I'm so very grateful. Get some dry clothes on."

The whole time this charade was going down, the doorman was making a studious perusal of a copy of the *Wall Street Journal* draped over the phone bank on his kiosk.

Klinger was back at the Hawse Hole within twenty minutes of his initial departure. The cab fare came to a mere sixteen dollars. Klinger threw the guy a twenty.

The OPEN sign in what used to be a window, along with the green neon martini glass above the front door, had been turned off. Klinger knocked, one-two, one-two, one. Bruce opened the door. Tommy pocketed the printed envelope without opening it. When Klinger offered the two twenties, Tommy told him to keep them. A double shot of Jameson anchored the C-note to the bar. Klinger had a sip before retiring to the head for an additional bump. They partied until dawn.

Thus it was that Klinger found himself fully clothed in bed in his hotel room about an hour after the sun came up, $247.19 to the good and listening to his heart beat erratically, almost as loud as the rain on the invisible window panes, but breathing easily, because that's the way speed-ball affected Klinger. He knew from nothing about other metabolisms.

After a while he sat up, took off his shoes, fluffed up the hopelessly thin pillow, and lay down again without bothering to remove the rest of his clothes.

He clasped his hands behind his head. So, Klinger thought with a contented sigh, it's about time a job went smooth.

Thus it was that Klinger almost had a coronary when, some three minutes later, Phillip Wong's cellphone rang in the breast pocket of his, Klinger's, jacket, and vibrated the thin layer of fascia between his damp shirt and his purring heart.

TEN

The ringtone crescendoed "Creation of Tron" by Wendy Carlos through his lingering chemistry, although Klinger might have assayed a longer sojourn on Planet Earth than the one for which he was slated without stumbling across that piece of information.

But really, in the event, the ringtone scared the piss out of him.

He fumbled at the breast pocket until he'd extracted the phone he hadn't known was there. He couldn't have handled it any more gingerly than if it had been a live scorpion. It was a smart phone, however, and as soon as it realized that it had received the attention for which it had signaled, it opened the connection. "Hello?" somebody said, and, "Phillip?" and, "Phillip, you are a genuine son of a bitch."

Klinger couldn't tell one end of the phone from the other. "Hello?" he responded uncertainly.

"What in heaven's name are you doing down here?"

"Down where?"

"In the Tenderloin!"

Klinger took umbrage. "How about I can't afford to be elsewhere?"

"Can't afford—? I've got your check. I—. Say, Phillip? Are you sick? You sound all nasally."

"Who wants to know?"

"What, you got software to disguise my voice instead of yours? This is Marci, you lummox."

"Marci, Marci . . ."

"I know you're not in the bar," the voice persisted, "because I've already looked in the bar."

This got Klinger's attention. He swung his legs over the edge of the bed. "What bar?"

"What is a hawse hole, anyway?"

"You're there now?"

"I minimized my exposure. It's only nine-fifteen in the morning and there's guys in there who look like they've been there since last week."

"That's the place all right."

"I'm on the sidewalk outside. WhereIz says you're close by."

Klinger tried to think faster than an app called WhereIz. Does electricity flow faster through dendrites or copper? How about speedballed dendrites? You mean, like, cryogenic copper? Perhaps it's at the metabolic level, Klinger did not permit himself to muse, that the vernacular breaks down.

"WhereIz, being a killer app, never fails," the woman's voice pointed out. "I am poised for when they go public. Hello?"

"I'm here," Klinger grudgingly admitted. Usually, in a rat trap like this, he took the trouble to ascertain the location of the fire escape. If he'd done his homework he might have been able to abandon the phone to the pillow and disappear. Maybe he could wing the phone out the window and onto the roof across the street? And she'd go look for it there? Maybe he could beat the phone to death with a chair leg? Maybe . . .

Maybe I should take the bull by the horns, Klinger abruptly thought: She mentioned a check.

"Say," he told the phone, using his most ingenuous phone voice, "I was just trying to figure out how to call somebody on this thing so I could maybe find out whose phone it is. I'm not too conversant with cellphones. I couldn't even figure out how to access the address book."

"It's probably password-protected. So for sure," the voice concluded, as if it hadn't already, "this is not Phillip."

"Whoever Phillip is, this isn't him." As if you didn't know, Klinger had already concluded. "And who was this, again?"

"I'm a friend of Phillip's. Maybe even his best friend, if not his only friend. So where did you find his phone?"

Good question. Klinger nodded thoughtfully. A logical question. "On the sidewalk," he said for no good reason. "Right in front of the bar, about seven o'clock this morning." He thought about it. "How did you know to look for this guy Phillip in the Hawse Hole?"

"This app, WhereIz," Marci enthused. "I told you. If you're connected to the phone, WhereIz brings up a map and erects a throbbing plood at your phone's location. Anywhere on earth. Even here."

"Huh," Klinger entertained an urge to repeatedly smash the phone between the upper edge of the bedside drawer box and the faceframe of the nightstand until it disintegrated into its constituent ploods.

"But you're not in the bar," Marci reminded him.

"I'm not in the bar," Klinger affirmed. "Although, statistically speaking?"

"Yes?"

"It's hard to believe you missed me."

"I see . . . I think." Marci sighed. "So where are you, if you're not in the bar?"

Wow, Klinger thought, that was most assuredly a sigh of impatient tenacity. This chick doesn't give a rat's ass about how much time I spend in the bar. Whereas I, myself, care exclusively about the time I spend there. We

JIM NISBET

are contrapositive propositions, she and I. Destined, no doubt, to cancel each other out.

He shook his head. That's silly.

At the very moment his mind articulated this adjective, Klinger shivered involuntarily. I gotta get a hot shower and a meal, he reminded himself.

"I'm upstairs," Klinger told the phone abruptly. "In the hotel."

She hardly missed a beat. "What room?"

For some reason, Klinger instinctively backpedaled. "Let's meet in the bar."

"No," Marci parried succinctly. "They still let people smoke in there."

"It is a shithole," Klinger agreed. "Hawse is a genteelism."

"And the hotel?" Marci persisted brightly.

"Not very distinguishable from ditto," Klinger warned her.

"Hey, pal," Marci said, "I'm out front, remember? How disillusioning could it be?"

"How soon I forget," Klinger muttered sourly. Frankie Geeze, he apostrophized, you fun-loving motherfucker, you surely didn't lose your touch inna joint. Klinger reflected a moment. It's stupid moves like your stupid move with the phone that got you in the joint in the first place. That, and your habit. As my old pal Georgie once happened to mention, Klinger my boy, Georgie happened to mention, I've known a lot of dippers in my day, and every last one of them was a hophead. It's got something to do with their nerves. They're usually pretty good at what they do, too, which is picking a pocket with an L-shaped length of wire. But I don't like them. Talented, skillful and smart they may be, and a lot of them are all those things, but every last one of them is *hincty*, cause every last one of them is a hophead, and a hophead don't care but about the one thing, and that's his dope.

96

I wonder, Klinger wondered, passing his thumb back and forth along the edge of the phone, if this is what Georgie meant by hincty. Surprising me with this phone was a fucking lame thing to do.

"Pardon?"

"What's the room number?" Marci repeated.

"Say," Klinger replied, "what's that noise? Is this phone tapped or something?"

"Aside from the fact that our government can tap any phone it wants to tap," Marci replied, "what noise?"

"That noise," Klinger said. "You don't hear it?"

"What's it sound like?" Marci said, humoring him, albeit not without a trace of impatience.

"Beeee," Klinger said, making with a high-pitched tone. Then he added a lower-pitched one. "Oop."

"Your battery's low," Marci responded without hesitation. "Quick, what's the room number?"

Klinger drew a breath. Then: "Three thirty-five. Take the stairs all the way up."

"How do I get in?"

"Next to the bar entrance there's a piece of plywood nailed over a window and covered with chicken wire and rebar and it's all painted gray. To the left of that there's a door, painted ditto?"

"I see it. Yech."

"The button's painted over, high up and to the right of the corner of the casing. A guy on the second floor will buzz you in. Tell him you're from Social Services—." The phone went dead. "—Hello?"

Klinger looked at the screen. BATTERY LOW was all that appeared on it. As he watched, the image faded, the phone emitted a pathetic peep, and the screen went black.

Huh.

Klinger dropped the useless phone onto the pillow.

Klinger considered his circumstances. His clothes were still wet, there was this dead phone, and there were $247.19.

End of story.

But now a visitor. He shivered. He hadn't had a visitor . . . He couldn't remember when he'd had a visitor. Even in jail, he hadn't had a visitor. Especially in jail. Other than which, it had been a very long time since he'd had a place to be visited in. He shivered again. Clean and dry clothes would be nice. Let's deal with the visitor, then clean and dry clothes will be the chore, and maybe a change of venue if I can get my money back, fat chance.

He considered the phone. Anyway, he leveled with himself, it's this phone that's getting visited, not me. She didn't even ask about that guy . . . Phillip. One el or two? No matter. It's the phone she's after. Not one el or two el Phillip, but this phone. Dead or alive, Klinger thought, referring to the phone, because Klinger didn't give a rat's ass about Phillip either. Charged or not. What's in a phone, anyway? Phone numbers?

Maybe there's a buck in it?

Klinger touched the dead cellphone. He'd never owned one. But certainly he'd heard that they'd evolved to the point where they'd pretty much become computers. He knew that Mary Fiducione had been able to quit her day job because of phones. He knew that street punks were jacking up tourists for their phones, not unlike they used to jack them up for sneakers or cameras. It wasn't hard. In fact, it was a lot easier than taking a pair of shoes off a sucker. You punch him in the face with one hand, grab his phone with the other, you book with both feet. Child's play. Children, in fact, were the ones perpetrating most of these kinds of crimes. It occurred to Klinger to wonder whether or not the cops knew about this WhereIz app. Get

in the cruiser with the victim, call his hijacked phone—
voilà. Another statistic.

No doubt somebody had already thought to call it
phonejacking.

Klinger looked around the room. Not even a closet. He
looked at the drawer in the bedside table. If he had a length
of duct tape he could park the phone on the back of the
drawer box, or underneath it. Fine. Send out for duct tape.
Next scenario would be . . . under the mattress? Please. In
the overhead light fixture? Try and be creative. He opened
the nightstand drawer, there to find a copy of *Dianetics:
The Modern Science of Mental Health*, and nothing else. He
closed the drawer.

In the end, Klinger slit an edge of the tinfoil which covered a pane of the room's window with his thumbnail and
slipped the phone into the slot so that it stood edgewise
on a mullion between glass and tinfoil. As concealment,
the result wasn't bad.

A knock. Klinger opened the door.

"Hello," she said.

"Hello," Klinger said. He stepped aside.

She came in.

"Sit down, sit down."

After a moment of uncertainty, she daintily perched
on the edge of the bed, a purse/briefcase thing on her knees.

"Don't worry," Klinger chuckled. "Cooties can't pen-
etrate polyester. Not right away, anyhow."

"This is silk," she corrected him matter-of-factly. She
stood, brushed the blanket with the flat of her hand, looked
at her hand, resettled herself on the bed.

"Kessler," the woman said, despite being unable to
resist taking in every forlorn detail of the room around her.
She held out the hand. "Marci Kessler."

"Klinger." He shook the hand, no knuckle-clutch,

no handles of beer steins involved. "Take your time," he encouraged her. "There's a lot to see."

She leveled her gaze at him. "I don't see a phone."

"Right down to business," Klinger nodded. "I like that. Do you have a charger?"

She shook his head. "How did you come by Phillip's phone again?" She made a little smile. "I forget."

Klinger nodded. "I found it on the sidewalk." He jerked his thumb at the headboard. "First thing this morning."

"First thing this morning . . ." she repeated thoughtfully.

Klinger contemplated his visitor. She was twenty-five, twenty-six. Short black hair well cut, clothes all black, the package looking understated but expensive. And the woman herself was . . . Klinger frowned. Was she good looking? He gave it a thought. Maybe so. Her intensity predominated, however, and, what, her focus? And, could she be on the defensive, too? Wrapped tight? But that's okay, Klinger wryly assured himself. She didn't come here to be attractive.

"I wonder . . ." she was saying.

"Yes?"

"I spoke with Phillip about nine o'clock last night. Maybe it was eight-thirty." She touched her phone. It made little blips. "Eight thirty-seven to nine oh five."

Klinger nodded. "Before it started raining."

"Oh," said she, affecting no interest whatsoever, "did it rain last night?"

Klinger assured her that it had been raining.

An awkward silence descended. Klinger could hear a television nattering, in one or another of the rooms around them, and he assumed she could hear it too. Out in the hall, a floorboard creaked. Four floors down, the street door closed with a bang.

"Look," she finally said. "Where's the damn phone?"

"It's here," Klinger told her.

"Aren't you going to give it to me?"

"It depends," Klinger frankly said, "on what the deal is."

"Deal? What deal?" she said faux-naively. "Did we have a deal? My friend lost his phone and you found it. You give it to me and I give it to him." She smiled. "Simple."

"Yeah," said Klinger.

"So what's this about a deal?" she asked.

"I don't know," Klinger said. "How about, how do I know you'll give it back to him?"

"You don't," she said. "You'll just have to trust me." Again with the smile. "Why wouldn't I give it back to him? After all," she said brightly, "I've got my own phone." She held it up.

"I didn't get where I got in life," Klinger said without irony, "by trusting people."

She deployed a little smile of disdain. "And where, exactly, have you gotten in life?"

"I'm still alive," Klinger declared with an offhand certainty. "It's a kind of triumph." He shrugged modestly. "For what it's worth."

After a thoughtful pause she said, "Trust is a strange thing, isn't it."

"Okay," Klinger said, as if patiently. "I bore easy." He took a stab in the dark. "This guy Phillip's beside the point. What's with the phone?"

She appeared to consider this. "Phillip . . . really needs his phone."

"Okay," Klinger lifted his hands. "I got all day. After all," he indicated their surroundings, "I live here."

Marci lifted an eyebrow.

"In other words," Klinger abruptly spelled it out, "I don't give a shit about Phillip or his phone, and I don't give a shit what's in it for him or for you. I was minding my own business until you got here, lady. Now all I want to know is, since I got this phone and you want it, what's in it for me?"

Marci batted her eyelashes. "Phillip's momentary gratitude?"

Klinger laughed in her face.

Marci's gaze did not flinch. "How about my momentary gratitude?"

Klinger looked at her. Her skin was flawless, her clothes clean, she smelled better than anything else in the room, and she was as dry as a seventeen-dollar martini. Klinger, on the other hand, was wet, cold, broke, alone, he stank of piss and adrenaline and other people's cigarette smoke and, to say the very least, he hadn't shaved and if he were to shave he'd have to buy the stuff to do it with and then he'd have to leave an island of stubble around the nick in his cheek until it healed.

"Give me a fucking break," he spat. And, in spite of himself, this declamation carried with it an unmistakable note of bitter sincerity.

I'm too tired for this, he told himself. And, he abruptly realized, whether or not this chick is smarter than I am, she's not tired at all.

He could see it in her eyes. She was intelligent, unafraid, fresh . . .

And predatory?

The thought gave Klinger some pause. He was used, in his milieu, to what you might call elevated levels of self-interest. But he'd never had the personal wherewithal to find himself elevated to the stature of *prey* in another man's eyes. Let alone, a woman's eyes. He'd never been worth the trouble. It was that simple. It had always been that simple. He liked it that simple.

"Look . . ." he suddenly began. Then he stopped. What the hell was happening to him? Had this woman, this complete stranger, abruptly deprived him of his nerve?

Her smile exuded confident certainty. "Exactly," she nodded. Otherwise, she didn't move. "Where's the phone?"

Klinger retrieved it from its pathetic hiding place and handed it over.

"As you said," she said after a moment's examination, "it's dead."

"Yes," Klinger agreed.

"And you don't have a charger."

"In my book," Klinger sighed, "a charger is an armored horse in *Ivanhoe*." He shook his head. "Do I look like a charger kinda guy?"

Marci declined the bait. "So, neither of us has a charger." She unzipped a side pocket of her purse and dropped the phone into it.

Klinger mused the situation over. On the one hand, he may have been letting slip an opportunity to further capitalize on last night's action. Something as simple as a reward, maybe. On the other hand, he might well be dodging the resulting beef. Manslaughter committed in the course of a felony, for example, if manslaughter there had been. Certainly the gravity of the latter seemed far greater than that of the former. So, once this person and that accursed phone were out of sight he would resume fretting over his existence in some other fleabag demesne and, so far as she would be concerned, effectively disappear forever. So far as he was concerned, this person will have become another live round dodged on the obstacle course of life.

"I . . . suppose you can always get your hands on a charger," Klinger suggested. "No doubt," he brightened, "your friend Phillip's got a charger. No?" he finished feebly.

Marci zipped the side pocket closed and set the purse/briefcase on the floor next to the bed. "No doubt." She stood and, much to Klinger's dismay, began to remove her jacket.

"Uh," said Klinger, nervous. "What now?"

After but a moment's hesitation Marci hung her

knee-length jacket on the lonely hook on the back of the entry door, dead center below a printed card headed RULES, chief among which figured NO VISITORS.

"Now?" Marci turned to Klinger and touched a button on her blouse.

"Now you may fuck me."

ELEVEN

A slight tremor clambered up the sternum, bifurcated at the manubrium, and dissipated. Nothing more. The only sounds specific to the room were the far-away laser battle peculiar to the rustle of silk, and the tinkle of bracelets. The only thing to look at was the sublunary lambence of her skin, unmarked by a past, all too present, presentimental, utterly incisive to the imagination. And what his imagination presented to Klinger was dread. If the specter of lust had arisen, it would have dissolved into weightless foam upon the beach of his feckless trepidation. But there was no lust. Only aversion. Only the abrupt thought of the cash in his pocket, only a sudden apprehension as to where, exactly, that pocket might be at the moment, what with a stranger in his room and all. Only the feeble light admitted to his cave by the exit to all else, a door, a portal, a vector created by the vacuum sucking him parched and drinkless into the greater world, a mere three or four days hence. Klinger lifted his hands and it may well have looked like a supplication. He even managed the word "please."

She paused in her undressing. "No need to beg," she smiled.

Klinger shook his head and made little waving motions with the palms of his hands.

Marci allowed the shoulders of her blouse to fall to her elbows. Her black brassiere seemed the tracery of indecipherable arabesqueries upon the ivory astrolabe of her skin.

His mind just short of flailing itself for a rationale, Klinger began again. "It's not . . ." he stammered, "I . . ."

A shadow of uncertainty flitted from one carefully sculpted eyebrow to another. "What is it, then?"

"It's just that . . . You have the phone," Klinger blurted.

She looked at her purse.

"Please!" Klinger exclaimed through clenched teeth. "Take it and go."

Was he begging? Perhaps she caught the tone of mendicity. Perhaps it was unmistakable, perhaps she'd heard it before. But the vein of this plea was different. She countered it with one of her own. She peeled the diaphanes of the brassiere from her breasts. "I'm getting married soon." One sleeve of the blouse slipped off her arm. "I want experience."

Klinger's head was shaking involuntarily, but the negative was volitional. "No." His hands fluttered as if feebly trying to wave off a wall as it fell on him. "I mean . . . I'm not . . . It's . . ."

Now she shook her head. "Everybody's got something to bring to the sexual feast," she assured him. "It's the nature of experience in the natural realm."

Klinger, still shaking his head, exhaled loudly. "This is not natural," was all he could think of to suggest.

The other sleeve slipped off the other arm. "It's the most natural thing in the world," she asserted with confidence. "And it only gets better with experience." She batted her eyes. "Or so I'm told."

"So—so," Klinger stammered, "why not practice with your . . . your intended?"

"He's too busy," she stated mater-of-factly. The blouse dropped to the floor. "I hardly ever see him."

"That . . . that's a shame," Klinger managed.

She took a step forward.

Klinger took a step backward.

Marci frowned, just a little, but she was also amused. "Are you serious?" she said, unable to repress a smile.

Klinger vigorously nodded.

Marci applied the fingertips of one hand to a corner of her mouth, as if considering Klinger's reticence.

Klinger, who had never experienced a migraine headache in his life, felt one coming on; it was if a slim blade were slowly entering the right hemisphere of his brain. He squinted one eye against it.

She moved one step closer. "What was your name?"

"Smith," Klinger told her involuntarily. He opened the eye. "I mean Klinger. It's Klinger."

Her hands had fallen to the zipper on the hip of her skirt. "You're not living up to it," she said huskily.

Klinger frowned. "I beg your—. Oh." He shook his head. "You mean, I'm not clinging very well."

She shook her head. "You're not clinging at all."

"Well," Klinger stipulated forthrightly, "perhaps you're not getting the message."

The zipper, an inch or two along its course, stopped its descent. "What's that supposed to mean?"

She looked alarmed. Klinger made the palms of his hands shape the air between himself and this strange woman, as if they were finding their way through spider floss. "Nothing, nothing," Klinger insisted. "It's just that I—. I . . ."

Now Marci's own enthusiasm began to wane. "It's just that you what?" she asked with apparent sincerity. "Come on." She pulled the zipper back to its public position. "You can tell me." She crossed her arms over her breasts and frowned. "Are we queer? Impotent? Dead?"

Klinger began to shake his head, but switched to nodding it. Then, reconsidering, he began to shake it again.

"Well?" she said. "Go ahead. Don't be afraid. You can't

shock me. As Vice President of Compliance, I've heard it all."

Klinger resolved to speak before she threatened him with therapy. "It's just . . ." he began.

Marci nodded.

"It's just that . . ." Klinger began again.

"Come on," she coaxed him.

"It's just that I don't give a shit," Klinger expostulated, and speaking with more energy than heretofore.

For once in the hour, Marci seemed taken aback.

"It's that simple," Klinger said, modulating his tone so as to sooth her. "And it's nothing personal. Honest."

Marci appeared to consider this.

"Trust me," Klinger told her, deliberately tamping the begging tone from his voice. "It's the way it is."

Marci watched the palms of her crossed arms as they smoothed her own breasts. "While it's true that I don't have much experience," she said, "which is what I was trying to glean, what little I do have is contravened by your professed reaction." She slipped the fingers of each hand beneath the upper seam of the respective cup of her brassiere and inhaled so that her breath hissed between her teeth. "Am I not to your liking?" she asked, watching him through slitted eyes.

Klinger bit his lip. She was nubile, for starters. She had beautiful skin and, for all he knew, she was a beautiful woman. Klinger bit the inside corner of his mouth. Experience would come, all right. But that wasn't Klinger's point. Klinger's point was that Klinger didn't give a shit. A point very difficult, if not impossible, to explain to anybody, let alone to this young woman. She, to whose every whim a large portion of the world's men would only be too happy to cater, could barely comprehend that the wages, as it were, of such as Klinger lay well beyond her ability to pay. Only profound experience of the type with which catalogue Klinger was all too familiar would grant to this woman, this girl, this . . . *foxy executive* a mere gleam of insight into the depth of Klinger's despair. If sexuality is an impulse toward life, it is precisely the impulse that the likes of Klinger long ago left behind, and assiduously avoid recultivating, for, to them, any impulse toward life, sex included, perhaps sex chief above all, serves only to prolong the agony; and, if you were really unlucky, exquisitely so.

"Put your clothes on," Klinger abruptly said. His voice carried an unexpected ring of authority, and it was sufficient to take Marci aback. Her complexion colored.

She let fall her hands, then extended her arms away from her hips, palms outward. "Do you not find me desirable?"

"I'm sure you're very beautiful," Klinger said quietly, his voice uninflected by so much as a particle of interest. "And no doubt your future husband will express himself accordingly."

She appeared to consider this. But watched him as she did so. "I've never had an orgasm," she suddenly announced.

While, to some people, this may seem a fine topic for discussion, Klinger found himself at the end of forbearance. Can of worms, he told himself. You're almost out of it. Don't go there. He pointed at the briefcase. "There's probably an app for that."

Poised for disappointment, Marci smiled. "Phones are getting good," she said. "But not that good."

A silence fell between them.

"I can't help you," Klinger finally said.

Marci looked at him, then looked around the room. Fourteen by twelve feet. Curtains, once beige, now brown, with finger smudges shoulder high. Tinfoil on the panes,

JIM NISBET

as perhaps a poor man's Faraday grid, intended to keep out evil radio signals along with the least soupçon of daylight; a sempiternally cold radiator below, and it, too, painted gray many times. A dirt-flocked light bulb on a cord dangled from the ceiling, and a beaded pull-chain dangled from that, with an odorless and faded pine-tree air freshener as finial. Gray carpet heading to black, its pile mostly shredded, even its formaldehyde leeched into the ambient fetor long since, let alone any comfort it might afford to stockinged feet. A brown haze deposited by cigarette smoke on the ceiling directly above the damp impression of a human on the bed's gray blanket. A bedside stand that held no clock, no book, no phone, no radio. The walls had been papered, painted, papered, then painted again, gray, gray, gray, into the layers of which many thumbtack holes revealed a long and fading trail of disappeared images, icons, photos, clippings, pinups, prayers, calendars. She turned back to Klinger. "Of all the places to find a man I can respect," she said at last. She retrieved her blouse from the floor, turned her back on him, set about getting dressed. "You've never had a decent woman in your life?" she said to the door.

"The more decent they were," Klinger answered without hesitation, "the sooner I ruined them. After that, they were nothing but trouble. In the end I realized that if I cut women out of my equation, I saved myself any number of difficulties. Them, too."

"And how long ago was that?" she asked the door.

Klinger snorted. "I have no idea."

She turned around. "How's this?"

"You're pretty with your clothes off, you're pretty with them on," Klinger offered.

She made a little grimace. "It's kind of you to say so. Now what?"

110

Klinger shrugged. Despite having been up all night, he no longer felt like sleeping. "Now I guess I'll get some coffee. After that, I'll visit the Goodwill, buy myself some dry clothes."

Marci put on her jacket. "How about some breakfast?"

This took Klinger aback.

"Know a place?"

Klinger nodded dumbly.

She glanced at the face of a little watch on the outside of the wrist that bore no bracelets. "We'll be able to buy a battery in about an hour."

Klinger blinked. "We?"

Marci nodded. "If Phillip's phone coughs up the information I need, there will be a reward for you."

"Reward ..." Klinger repeated, almost to himself. "What sort of reward?"

"Well," Marci smiled wryly, obviously gaining on her former confidence, "since you turned down the good stuff, how about a little cash money?"

"Money ..." Klinger said softly. "Oh, money ..."

"Jesus Christ." Marci made a little frown. "Is money another sign of life you abjure?" She shook her head with authority. "That just can't possibly be true. If you were to go about eschewing sex as well as money, you'd be as good as dead." She wagged a finger at him, so that the bracelets rattled. "If not dead in fact."

Klinger shook his head. "It isn't." Then he nodded. "It isn't a sign of life which I ..."

"Eschew," Marci prompted him.

"Dodge," he substituted. "Don't get me wrong," he continued, suddenly loquacious, "I like money. I really do. It's just that money is the bane of my existence. All my life," Klinger confirmed, "money has been the bane of my existence."

"Listen to me," Marci told him, suddenly all gravity. "You dear, dear man." She extended her hands toward him, palms down. Klinger's mouth fell open. She turned her palms up and waggled her fingers. "Come on," she said. Klinger blinked. She waited. Klinger covered her palms with his own. She clasped his hands with hers. She clasped them gently, but she clasped them firmly. She locked eyes with him "Are you listening to me?"

Klinger nodded.

"I can't hear you," she said, "Klinger," she added, using his name for the first time.

"I'm listening," he told her.

"Marci," she told him.

"Marci," he repeated.

"Look at me," she told him.

Klinger raised his eyes. It was the first time he'd looked another human being in the eye in a very long time. He didn't even go eyeball to eyeball with his own reflection—especially his own reflection. There's more than one reason they don't put mirrors in these rooms—. "I'm listening," he abruptly said.

"Money," Marci told Klinger in all sincerity, "should be the bane of other people's lives. Not yours." She gave their clasped hands a squeeze. "Other people's. Understand?"

Klinger watched her with amazement, and not a little alarm. What money? What other people? There was never any money. None. And there were no other people, not any to speak of, not any other people who counted, no people who counted at all.

At bottom, Klinger had no idea what she was talking about.

"Well," she said. "Do we understand one another?"

"Sure," Klinger nodded and lied. "Sure." He smiled woodenly. "Can I have my hands back?"

"Only if you promise me," she said earnestly, "that you will try to bring to bear what I have just told you upon your daily life, and especially," she squeezed the hands, "upon those around you."

Klinger watched her, askance, from under the ledges of his eyebrows. When she'd finished speaking, he moved his head through a figure eight. It might have been a token of hasty agreement. It might have been a recalcitrant shudder of denial. It might have been a fly in an orgone box, desperate to escape.

"Okay," Marci said. "Good." She released his hands, and paused to smile before she retrieved her purse/briefcase from the floor next to the bed.

"Let's go get some breakfast."

TWELVE

Outside, the rain was coming down.

"Listen," Klinger told her when they'd descended to the street. "I need a drink."

She glanced at her watch. "It's ten-thirty in the morning."

Klinger regarded her with frank amazement. "What's that got to do with it?"

She lifted her hands.

Down at the end of the bar, the two guys in flannel shirts had laid off the mumblety-peg. Midway along the bar the old man had his usual seat, and Bruce was behind the plank, ringing up a sale.

They took a pair of stools adjacent to the old man.

"Oh, my goodness," Marci said, as they settled in.

Klinger, who had taken up a *Chronicle* that lay on the bar, intact but for its sports section, looked at her. She slid her eyes toward the bartender, who wore, as Klinger soon observed, boots of the type with a buckled strap over the instep, a pair of chaps, a vest, and a high-visored officer's cap, all black, all leather, and all by itself with no other apparel.

"It must be Saturday," the old man said, turning a page in the sports section without looking up.

"Friday," Bruce said to the cash register. "I'm starting early."

"You think he'd take the time to visit a tanning booth."

Bruce waggled his ass. "My regulars like their buns untoasted." He keyed the old-fashioned register without

turning around. The drawer slid open with an indefatiga-
ble ca-ching.

"Hirsute and wan," the old man qualified.

Bruce turned to spin a pair of cocktail napkins onto
the bar in front of his newly arrived customers. "What's
your pleasure?"

Klinger looked up from the paper. "Go ahead," Marci
said. "It's on me."

"Grog." Klinger returned his attention to the newspaper. "Jameson double."

"What's that?" she asked.

Bruce set a coffee mug on the bar in front of Klinger
and explained the drink as he built it. "Hot water, juice of
half a lemon, sugar because there's never been any honey
at the Hawse Hole other than yours truly, and whiskey."
He centered the coffee mug on its coaster. "It's medicinal."

Marci had been watching attentively. When Bruce had
finished she said, "That looks good. May I try one?"

"Take that one," Klinger said, as he opened the Metro
section.

Marci shook her head. "Too much whiskey. Could you
make me one with half that?"

"Absolutely." Bruce placed a mug in front of Marci and
started over.

Klinger, meanwhile, had found something to read.

SAN FRANCISCO—Passersby called police to the scene
of an apparent double mugging in North Beach on
Thursday night.

Authorities convened onto the 900 block of
Montgomery St., between Broadway St. and Pacific Ave. at
11:16 p.m. where they found the two men unconscious. A
passing pedestrian, one of a number to call 911, could pro-
vide no information about the two victims. Twenty-dollar

bills were strewn about the scene, a police spokeswoman said, apparently overlooked by the mugger or muggers in their haste.

Emergency vehicles removed the victims, both men, to St. Francis Memorial Hospital, where one of them was pronounced dead at 1:45 a.m. The survivor remains in critical condition. Police and hospital authorities are withholding identification pending notification of next of kin.

Witnesses to the incident are encouraged to call a confidential tips line . . .

Klinger skimmed the balance of the Metro section. There was no mention of a convenience store stickup.

He reread the double-mugging item.

Shit, Klinger said to himself, as he folded the paper. Could it be the cops didn't find Frankie's wire?

He watched steam spiral up off the golden surface of his toddy and shook his head. Once they ran his prints, it wouldn't make any difference.

Which is the dead guy, which the survivor?

He passed his now lemon-fragrant palm over his grizzled face.

Marci's phone rang. She plucked it from her purse, looked at the screen, stood off her stool, excused herself, and headed for the front door. "That's a polite little lady you got there," the old man said to his sports section, "who don't mind putting some distance between her neighbors and her phone conversation."

"Yeah," Klinger said, not half paying attention. "She's like that."

For sure the cops will make Frankie whether he survived or not. Klinger took a tentative sip. The toddy was good and it was hot and he took some consolation in it, but he took further solace in a pair of twinned facts. To wit, if Frankie hadn't survived, Klinger's contribution to Thursday's debacle would remain unknown; if Frankie had survived, however, he wouldn't tell the cops a thing. Frankie was a professional. Klinger's anonymity was assured.

Dead or alive, on the other hand, Frankie Geeze was done.

Bummer.

Klinger wrinkled his lips and recalled a case in point.

Several years before, a witness noticed a bicyclist exit the Broadway Tunnel, heading west, at two-thirty in the morning.

Ten minutes later, at Steiner and Jackson, high atop Pacific Heights, three pedestrians in a crosswalk toppled the cyclist in an attempt to rob him.

The bicyclist, however, hit the pavement rolling, came up in a crouch holding a pistol in both hands, and precisely drilled his assailants once each. Then he sprinted into the darkness of Alta Plaza Park, diagonally across the intersection, never to be seen again.

The commotion drew the attention of someone six stories up in a building overlooking the intersection, who called the cops.

One of the three assailants died on the spot. A second was grievously wounded. The third, also wounded, helped the second man half a block down Steiner, where they got into a pickup truck. The driver managed to back the truck out of its perpendicular parking place but only got a block away before he crashed it into a row of parked cars.

Meanwhile, before the cops arrived, a fifth party happened onto the scene, noticed the bicycle lying in the crosswalk, and stole it.

When the cops showed up, the observant neighbor met them in the street, mentioned the theft of the bicycle, pointed out the body in the crosswalk, and led the authorities down the hill to the crashed pickup truck. In its cab they found a dead passenger and the guy behind the wheel wounded and unconscious.

Net result? The surviving mugger found himself slapped with two counts of murder, which, having been committed in the course of another felony, the attempted robbery, made him liable to special or aggravating circumstances—a capital offense. It made no difference whatsoever that it was somebody else who shot the surviving suspect and his two partners. It didn't even make a difference if the survivor had no previous strikes. The surviving suspect took the fall.

The cops put out the word that they'd like very much to talk with the cyclist, as well as to the man who stole the bicycle.

Nobody came forward.

If Frankie Geeze were already dead? He was better off.

Klinger sipped his drink.

Which leads us . . .

Klinger contemplated the second toddy on the counter.

Which leads us to that extra cellphone.

"If I'm a lousy hour late to work," Marci said, resuming her seat, "it's like the whole company falls apart."

"Is it your company?"

"Not yet," she said. "Ow." She leaned back and glanced under the bar. "There's hooks under there."

"For your purse," Klinger pointed out.

"How civilized." She lifted her briefcase/purse and hung it under the bar, directly in front of her knees. "Perfect." She frowned. "What's this?"

Klinger laid his hand on her forearm.

Marci looked at him.

Klinger could have told her that, if she asked, Bruce

would give her eight inches of duct tape with which to adhere her pistol or knife or eight-ball bindle to the underside of the bar, just in case the cops showed up and frisked everybody in the joint. But he merely shook his head.

"Guy said he'd be back," the old man quietly told his sports section.

Klinger gently guided Marci's arm until its hand was above the bar. "Your drink is getting cold."

Marci tried her drink. "Mmm. Good." She tried it again, then put it down. "How can you drink at this hour?"

Klinger drained his own mug. "What hour?" He set the empty on the bar. Bruce pointed. It was an interrogative gesture.

"Finish mine," Marci said, before Klinger could react.

Klinger shrugged.

"Nudge?" Bruce asked him.

"Bruce," Klinger declared, "you're a lot more sensitive than your costume would suggest."

Bruce topped off Marci's toddy with whiskey and returned the bottle to its shelf under the back bar. "Like you know from sensitive."

"Where's this breakfast place?" Marci asked, as Klinger downed half the repurposed toddy.

Klinger paused to swallow, then downed the second half. "Pine and Hyde." He placed the second empty on the bar next to the first. "I was there just . . ." He frowned. "Yesterday? It doesn't seem possible."

Marci, repossessing her purse, looked up. "Where?"

Klinger repeated the coordinates.

Marci pulled a collapsed umbrella from the purse and smiled. "What a coincidence."

"Yes?" Klinger asked without interest.

"Phillip," Marci said, "is in St. Francis Memorial."

Klinger hesitated. "The phone guy?"

Marci nodded.

Klinger frowned. "He's in St. Francis?"

"Right there on the same corner," she nodded. "It's the whole block."

Klinger pointed at her purse. "Is that what that call was about?"

"It came up."

So Frankie Geeze is dead.

"I've got his room number." Marci evinced an enthusiastic smile. "He'll be so pleased to get his phone back."

"Yeah." Klinger looked at the folded *Chronicle*. "Want your paper?" he asked the old man.

Ostensibly absorbed in the sports section, the old man grunted.

"I guess that's a negative," Klinger said.

"Did you check the Lotto?" the bartender asked.

"You play that shit?"

"Every day," Bruce said. "Give it here."

Klinger handed Bruce the paper. "What's he doing in the hospital?"

"No idea," Marci said. "But we're going to find out."

Klinger stared at her. "We?"

"Sure," She pushed a button on the umbrella and its handle trebled in length. "Why not?"

"Well," Klinger suggested, "how about I don't even know the guy."

"But you found his phone," Marci reasoned. She pushed another button and the handle blossomed in front of her. "A guy like Phillip?" She shouldered her purse. "His phone is his life. He's got everything in there. And what he doesn't have in there?"

Klinger waited glumly.

"It's in the cloud, and his phone can access the cloud."

"The cloud . . ."

Marci pointed straight up.

Klinger lifted his eyes halfway to the ceiling before he thought to discover a gleam of hope. "Even if it's dead?"

Marci looked at him. "That's right. I'd forgotten." She shot a cuff and looked at her watch. "We need a charger. Better yet, we need a battery. Better yet—both. Hold this." She offered Klinger the umbrella.

If I'd gone ahead and fucked her, Klinger was thinking, we might not be having this conversation. He took the umbrella. I take that back, oh yes we would.

Marci produced her own phone and began to tap its screen. "Okay . . ." she said to herself. "What's . . ." She drew Phillip's phone from her purse, studied its case, turned it in the light to discern its model number. "Okay . . ." She returned the dead phone to her purse and tapped her screen. "There's a phone store at . . . No . . . How about . . ." She nodded. "Proximity . . . Hang on . . . I know there's an app for this . . ."

"It's called the brain," Klinger submitted.

"Van Ness and Clay," Marci nodded and smiled. "Okay. That's pretty close." She tapped the screen. "They open at eleven."

"Van Ness and Clay?" Klinger almost whined. "That's, like, twelve blocks from here."

"Thirteen," said the old man, looking up from his paper.

"Really?" Bruce said to the cash register. "I'd have said eleven."

"Whatever," Klinger said testily. "It's pissing down rain, and I'm already wringing wet."

"We'll take a cab." Marci tapped her phone a couple of times and held it to her ear.

"Listen," Klinger told her. "I'd like to get by the Goodwill for a change of clothes."

"And it's where?" Marci asked over the phone.

"The big one's at Van Ness and Mission," Klinger told her.

"That's South Van Ness," the old man said to his newspaper.

"He's right," Bruce said to his cash register.

"You heard them," Klinger said.

"Will it take long?" Marci asked.

"Fifteen minutes," Klinger assured her.

"Yes, we're at Ellis at Hyde, please," Marci told her phone, adding, after a pause, "Clay and Van Ness, waiting, then Mission and South Van Ness, waiting, then to St. Francis Memorial, at Hyde and Pine." She turned off the phone.

"They're on the way," she said brightly.

THIRTEEN

Klinger and Marci exited the Hawse Hole, on Hyde just below Ellis, at ten-thirty in the a.m.

Marci peered beneath the catenary of her umbrella's rim and through the smoking rain at the name above the bar's entrance. "How come everybody calls it the Horse Hole, when it's spelled h-a-w-s-e? Is that a gay thing?"

"Very likely." Klinger had no more set foot on a boat than he'd wondered about the name of the bar.

Marci donned a pair of shades whose blind spot had been co-opted by their designer's faux gold initials. "I expect to devote time to alternate cultures after I cash out and take early retirement."

Klinger only stared at her.

"Get under here," she said. "You'll catch your death."

Klinger had never heard the word hypothermia, but it was true that he was flirting with it.

"Here's our cab."

A taxi painted entirely green, with an overlay of advertising, glided silently to the curb.

"How'd you do that?" Klinger thought to inquire, as he opened the back door.

She ignored the question. "You first." She followed Klinger into the back seat, folded the umbrella and gave it a shake over the gutter before she closed the door. "Van Ness and Clay," she told the driver. "A phone store."

With a glance at his side-view mirror, the driver made as if to pull back into traffic, but a klaxon, violent and unyielding, persuaded him otherwise. To the extent that he swerved back to the right and managed to stop before he piled into a Mercedes parked in front of the Tuolumne Meadows Residential Hotel, he appeared to be an excellent driver.

"Son of a bitch," the cabbie declared in an objective tone. He grabbed a crucifix, which dangled from a rosary wrapped around the stalk of the rear-view mirror, and touched it to his lips.

Klinger and Marci, as yet unbelted, found themselves piled against the respective seat backs in front of them.

"Buckle up," the cabbie admonished.

A wall of malarial yellow eclipsed the light in the driver's side windows, and a wave of rainwater lifted up between the two vehicles, drenching the glass.

The cabbie checked his rear-view mirror and tried again.

This time they made it.

Marci started over. "Van Ness and Clay. A phone store."

"Got it the first time," the cabbie told his rear-view mirror.

"Speaking as someone who has nearly been impaled by her own umbrella," Marci replied politely, "it's nice to be dealing with a professional."

"Them Hummers," the cabbie said to his windshield, "are an affliction, a scourge, a bane, and expensive."

"Indeed," Marci agreed. "Comfortable, too. Heated seats. Individual thermostats. Plus, they make me feel safe. When I'm on the inside of one of them, I mean," she clarified, "I feel safe."

"This baby here," the cabbie said, patting the dashboard, "runs on pure corn."

"Corn," Klinger repeated.

"Yeah," the cabbie assured the mirror. "Like the news."

"Would that be . . ." Marci asked tentatively, "genetically modified corn?"

The cabbie had a gold tooth, and now it twinkled in the mirror. "Is there any other kind?"

Marci looked out her window, and chewed her lip. "Good question."

"Actually," the cabbie said to his mirror, "the correct answer is, Not for long."

Klinger, paying little attention to the conversation, was looking out his own window. It seemed that as many as a third of the storefronts on this stretch of Hyde Street were vacant. Some had signs—For Sale or Lease, All or Part, 100-2,000 Sq. Ft., Will Build To Suit—but many were boarded up and painted over with that universal gray, up to which color miscellaneous used buckets of paint will sum, when mixed together at the behest of harried landlords cited by a city that no longer has the tax base to deal with graffiti abatement on its own. Not that Klinger knew any of this. All he saw was rain-glistened desuetude.

"You know," the taxi driver was saying, "I did a calculation."

"In my line of work," Marci said, as she watched her side of the world go by, "I do a lot of spreadsheets."

"You're an unusual woman," the cabbie said to his mirror. "I can see that."

Marci nodded vaguely.

"People talk about how many Hummers it would take to pave the planet," the cabbie said.

"They do?" Marci frowned.

"Sure," said the cabbie. "When you consider their footprint, you wouldn't think it would calculate out to too damn very many of them. Am I right?"

"I don't know," said Marci. "What is their footprint?"

"Ninety-seven point four square feet," the cabbie

promptly replied. "Not including winches, tow packages, cowcatchers and other extenuating devices and after-market add-ons."

Marci looked at the rear-view mirror. "There are towns in California where it's illegal to construct outbuildings that big."

"You're beginning to see the picture," the cabbie assured the mirror.

"And the footprint of the planet?" Marci asked.

"Five hundred and ten million square kilometers."

"Which—," Marci began.

"Which needs to be converted into square feet," the cabbie replied impatiently, an edge creeping into his voice.

"Take a right on Turk," Marci interjected, an edge of firmness in her own voice.

The cabbie took a right from the middle lane and cut off another taxi attempting to take its own right. The other taxi was painted yellow, and its horn sounded, long and aggrieved.

"Fucker's still burning fossil fuel," the cabbie observed with contempt. "Fuck him."

"And right on Van Ness," Marci directed.

"Look," the cabbie said without hesitation. "Didn't you tell the dispatcher that you want me to wait?"

"Yes."

"Okay. Consider the following. That phone store you're interested in is on the west side of Van Ness, and it's maybe three doors down from the corner. You want me to drop you on the east side of the street, so you have to wait for the light to let you cross six lanes of Van Ness in the pissing-down rain?"

Marci didn't even think about it. "No."

"That's right. So I should continue on to Franklin, turn north, pass over Clay to Washington, take a right on

Washington, right again on Van Ness, and wait in the bus zone out front of the telephone store, aimed southbound for our next stop, which," he touched the side of his head, "is at South Van Ness and Mission Street."

"Brilliant," Marci had to agree.

"Hey," the cabbie stipulated at his rear-view mirror, "I'm a professional."

"Of that, I am reassured," Marci declared.

Turk is one-way going west. The cabbie crushed an orange, as they say, then dove into the right lane on the other side of Van Ness. Two more horns sounded.

"You see?" Marci said to Klinger, as she gripped with both hands the back of the seat in front of her. "Some people have fun while they're working."

What persuades this woman, Klinger scowled at his own window, to presume to share these trivialities with me?

"Converting to square feet and dividing," the cabbie said, casting a glance to his left as he ran the red light and took a right onto Franklin, "we get five hundred and sixty-three trillion."

Marci looked at Klinger. Klinger wasn't having any part of this conversation. Or monologue. Or whatever it was. "I'll bite." Marci turned back to the mirror. "Five hundred trillion what?"

"Hummers to pave the planet," the cabbies said to the mirror. He pointed toward the floorboards. "This planet," he added. "So there's nowhere's near enough."

"Enough what?"

"Hummers."

"Ohhh," said Marci. "That does indeed seem like a vast deal of Hummers." She elbowed Klinger. "Isn't that a lot of Hummers, darling?"

Klinger moved even closer to his own door. These chatty humanoids were making rainy-day sociopathy easy this morning. If it hadn't been streaming with rain, just on the other side of this thickness of glass, he might have bolted into the traffic on Franklin Street.

"I need to get into the left lane as we go north," the cabbie said, "or else we'll wind up in the parking garage underneath Whole Foods watching housewives in SUVs flipping each other off."

"We're in a bigger hurry than that," Marci assured him, "with a great deal more important things to attend to."

"I couldn't agree more." The cabbie merged his vehicle all the way to the left lane. "Plus it's an ugly side of humanity you don't ordinarily like to admit is there to be witnessed, down there in that garage. They should have a three-headed dog guarding it."

Sure enough, as they rose up the hill from Pine to California, a line of SUVs queuing to access the entrance to an underground parking garage blocked the right lane.

The cabbie and Marci both pointed at the rear-view mirror and said, "A professional."

A small but measurable amount of bile raised to within a couple of inches of Klinger's trachea. He choked it down with a snarl, aided by the thought that one head is plenty.

But the cabbie was indeed a professional and, soon enough, his green taxi was blocking a bus zone within a few doors of a phone store on Van Ness.

"I'll be right back," Marci told them. She placed her hand on the door handle and looked back at Klinger. "Do you need anything?"

Klinger nodded yes at his fogging window but made no other answer, as what he needed isn't to be found in a phone store.

Marci opened the door, flared the umbrella, exited.

Klinger and the cabbie waited. The rain pounded on the roof. A certain funk began to lift off Klinger's soaked clothing, to cloy the atmosphere inside the taxi. Without a word, the driver cracked his window.

Unable to pull into the bus zone, a bus pulled up beside the cab, blocking in turn the traffic behind it. Horns sounded, and the bus returned the compliment. The cabbie, touching buttons on his onboard computer, ignored them all.

A guy in a drenched T-shirt and a wheelchair rolled backward along the sidewalk, past Klinger's window. The front end of the bus groaned and knelt down, like a camel, and its doors opened. Its front steps converted into a ramp and flattened onto the streaming pavement. Rain fell upon the diamond plate treads with a fury that rebounded droplets a foot into the air. The guy in the wheelchair made his way forward, to the front of the cab, and began pounding on its fender with a gloved fist. The cabbie looked up from his computer, grunted, put the cab in reverse, checked all three of his rear-view mirrors, then backed up until the guy in the wheelchair could drop off the curb between the front bumper of the cab and the rear bumper of a Chevy Blazer, so as to get a straight run at the bus ramp. He wore a Giants baseball cap and water shot off its bill sufficiently to clear his knees, but not his unlaced sneakers, each of which was poised to receive its cascade by a rubber pad on a stainless steel stalk. On his second attempt, he got the chair properly aligned and drove it onto the ramp. The ramp lifted up and the wheelchair rolled into the bus. Before the ramp was properly retracted, the bus took off with a roar, angling into the southbound lane so that water shot off its redeveloping steps, and their forward corner took out the left rear taillight on the Blazer, and left a long, tapering fissure in the sheet metal of its left rear quarter panel.

When the bus had departed, the cabbie shifted into forward and closed the gap between the cab's front bumper and the Blazer, before reverting to the study of his onboard computer. The pounding on the taxi roof increased to a roar, then decreased to a pounding again, as a curtain of rain passed north along Van Ness Avenue. The taxi's radio squawked. A voice called out an incomprehensible address. Another voice said "Bingo." The radio went silent. The cabbie touched buttons on the onboard computer. Another bus arrived, stopped, disgorged a passenger, and departed, followed by dozens of cars and trucks. After another fifteen minutes the streetside passenger door opened, Marci sat sideways into the seat, collapsed the umbrella, and closed the door.

"Jesus Christ." She pulled a little box from a plastic bag and showed it to Klinger. "They have *one guy* working in there." Klinger nodded dully. "And now," she said over the seat back, as she began to open the flaps on the box, "the Goodwill at South Van Ness.

"Hmmm." The cabbie levered the machine into reverse, backed up a few feet, and studied his side-view mirror. "That's on the northeast corner. And you want me to wait again, am I right?"

"We want you to wait again," Marci confirmed. "You are right."

"So maybe I'll take a left at Grove, cut down Polk, cross over Market to Tenth, take a right on Mission and a right on South Van Ness. Almost that entire block above Mission is a bus zone. All you'll have to do is get out of the cab and make a dash for the front door. Just like here."

"You're a genius," Marci said.

"Yelp me," the driver said.

"You know what you want?" she said to Klinger, without looking up from her study of the package in her hand.

Klinger roused himself from his torpor. "Something thermal."

"Here." She produced a couple of twenties and folded his hand over them. "If you get something presentable, I'll take you to a presentable place for lunch."

Klinger looked at the money and looked at her. He said nothing, but he kept the money.

She made a little smile, sat back in her own corner, and watched the wet world go by.

The cabbie made good on his route, although it took two light changes to make the left onto Grove. By the time they pulled into the bus zone in front of the Goodwill, the meter read fifty-two dollars.

The Goodwill at the corner of Mission and South Van Ness is the biggest one in San Francisco. Before the so-called recession, it reliably turned over its inventory on a weekly basis. A few months into the so-called recession, it was churning the better part of its inventory on a daily basis.

Even so early, the place was mobbed. A couple of beautiful easy chairs and a couch flanking the double front doors were occupied by three people who obviously were there for no other reason than to get out of the rain. A guy on the customer side of the computer counter (the San Francisco Goodwill store at Mission and South Van Ness has a dedicated computer department) was holding forth on the virtues of DOS WordStar. No clerk on the other side of the counter paid him heed. Women were speed-dialing their way through racks of dresses and blouses, men were doing the same in the pants department. The clatter of crockery was almost deafening. Klinger took up a position behind the guy methodically looking at every pair of pants in menswear and, soon enough, a nice pair of lined woolen trousers turned up in Klinger's size. Ditto the shirt department, where he found a flannel item with long sleeves, ditto jackets, where he lucked into a navy pea coat of quilted wool complete with an anchor etched into each of its big blue buttons. New, this coat alone would cost well over a hundred bucks. Finally, in the bottom of a large carton full of hats, he turned up a dark blue woolen watch cap, a perfect match to the coat. In short order he scooped up a pair of thick woolen socks, a steeply discounted "Republicans for Voldemort" T-shirt, and a pair of summer weight Madras shorts to stand in for underwear. Altogether, he'd assembled an ideal foul-weather outfit. For shoes, however, he had to make do with a pair of high-top pseudo-fawn disco boots, each with a zipper on its instep and no tread whatsoever. But they fit over the wool socks.

The man ahead of Klinger in the register line was diminutive of stature, and he dressed sharp. His white linen trousers, belted high, were creased, as was his shirt, whose blacks limned a pattern of white geese merging into their contrapositives. Raindrops beaded the high gloss of his ebony shoes as if each were the hood of a black limousine.

The girl at the cash register scanned the barcodes of each of the man's purchases—a pair of dissimilar wine glasses, an Arizona! souvenir ashtray shaped like a saguaro cactus, a guide to Rocky Mountain wildflowers, a Pedro Infante DVD.

As the clerk bagged the last item, she read the total off the register. "Eight ninety-nine, sir."

The man perfunctorily patted his breast pocket and searched the pockets of his trousers, back to front, until he came up with a carelessly folded hundred-dollar bill, which he offered to the cashier with a modest shrug.

The clerk looked at the bill. "I can't do that, sir."

Shortstuff rubbed the bill between thumb and forefinger suggestively, as if he meant it for the girl, and as if maybe she wouldn't have to work too hard to earn it. If his expression betrayed nothing, the gesture came on lascivious.

"I'm sorry, sir," the cashier explained patiently. "I can't accept any bill larger than a twenty."

As if just noticing the line behind him, Shortstuff showed his bill to Klinger.

Klinger, who had maybe fifteen twenties on him, looked into the face of the customer with the C-note. The eyes were dead. Klinger made no move toward the cash in his pocket, and said nothing. If Klinger weren't abiding by a certain code, by which he wouldn't bust this guy's hustle, he might have been insulted at the net's being cast his way.

Behind Klinger, a woman said cheerily, "I have it, I think." The man's eyes skimmed over Klinger like a pair of shucked oysters sliding off a tray. Klinger turned, too, as did the clerk. Nobody said a word.

The third person in line was a woman with gray hair. She wore a floor-length tie-dye dress under a wool sweater, each of whose antler buttons faced a threaded loop of braided hair, possibly harvested from the six or eight reindeer circumnavigating her ribcage. She placed a one-dollar copy of an illustrated book titled *Deities of the Hindu Kush* on the counter while she fingered a twenty, a ten, a five, and two ones out of a chamois wallet embroidered with a tomahawk and an eagle feather.

If this isn't somebody's slaphappy grandmother, thought Klinger, she's missing a good chance.

Don't do it, Klinger might have advised the woman. As, indeed, the girl at the cash register might have advised as well. But, as it was, neither of them spoke. The girl had seen this a thousand times, no doubt, or maybe she really didn't understand what was going on and just followed the rules. Shortstuff stood as if he had all day to get the bread for his next fix. Or maybe he just had his eye on a pair of ninety-dollar shoes.

"Nope," the grandmother announced, apologetically showing her thirty-seven dollars to anybody who might have been interested, which was everybody. "Wishful thinking," she added with a chuckle. And, excepting the pair of singles, her money went back into her wallet.

Klinger reverted his eyes forward. Shortstuff was already looking at the clerk. "I can hold your purchases until closing time," she suggested, her expression neutral.

"There's a bank," Klinger volunteered, and pointed helpfully. "Right across Mission."

"Yeah," Shortstuff said, as if begrudgingly. "There is."

The clerk gathered the mouth of the shopping bag. "We close at five," she said, setting the bag on a shelf under the register counter. She moved her eyes toward Klinger. "Next, please."

As it happened, the front door was twenty feet beyond the cash register. As the clerk scanned his own purchases, Klinger watched the sharply dressed short guy pause at the front door. Beyond the glass, pedestrians scurried in driving rain. Only now did the customer thoughtfully pocket the hundred-dollar bill and apply himself to a quick study of a canister full of wet umbrellas, just inside the entrance. He selected a colorful example from among its black brothers, pushed open the front door. The umbrella opened over Shortstuff's head as he gained the sidewalk, displaying, as he turned, the logo of the Pebble Beach Country Club.

The Bank of America to which Klinger had referred was directly across Mission Street, to the left of the front door of the Goodwill store.

The sharply dressed little man under the stolen umbrella took a right and disappeared into the rain.

The bill came to fifty-six dollars, so that Klinger had

to kick in some of his own money toward the purchase. This chafed him.

Receipt in hand, Klinger nicked a bath towel and repaired to a changing booth. There he shucked his soaked duds onto the floor with a good riddance, dried himself off, having donned the newly purchased ensemble, moved his money from a wet pocket to a dry one, and departed.

The cab was right where he'd left it.

The meter read sixty-eight dollars.

"Okay," Marci was saying to her phone as Klinger re-entered the back seat. "Later. Hey," she said, putting her phone away. "Looking sharp."

"And toasty." Warm and more or less dry, feeling somewhat human and communicative, despite his ass prickling where it had been exposed to damp fabric for too long, Klinger essayed his most sociable inducement: "How about a drink?"

"How about breakfast first?" Marci chided him.

"How about both?" Klinger countered.

"Man," Marci chuckled. "Are you sure you're not some kinda *hombre de negocios*?"

Outside of *chiva* and *adiós* Klinger understood very little Spanish; but he knew from *man of business*, as it happened, for this was hardly the first time someone had made fun of his commercial acumen. Also not for the first time, Klinger found himself wondering about what he perceived as the strange relationship between business acumen and misanthropy.

Marci showed Klinger Phillip's cellphone. "Notice anything?"

Klinger shrugged. "The screen's illuminated."

"Very good," Marci nodded. "Can you read it?"

Klinger varied his head's distance from the screen and its angle to the available light.

"Well?" Marci asked impatiently.

"Enter Password," Klinger read aloud.

Marci dropped the phone into the mouth of her brief-case/purse.

"Goddammit," she pronounced.

FOURTEEN

The cabbie had whiled away Klinger's absence gleaning figures and statistics via the internet via the virtual keyboard on his cellphone, thence feeding them to a handheld scientific and graphing calculator.

"So," the cabbie had announced as Klinger opened the curbside door, "given that it's going to take some five hundred and sixty-three trillion Hummers to pave the planet?"

"Sure," Marci said, addressing her rain-swept window.

"And pegging," the cabbie continued, "the standard length of a Hummer at sixteen point nine six feet, exclusive of bikeracks and winches?" He thumped the display window of the calculator with a forefinger. "Thirty-seven times ten-to-the-sixth trips to the moon and back." He nodded. "That's round-trips, baby." He sucked a tooth. "If you could drive a single Hummer at the speed of light in order to take all them round-trips?" He worked his two machines: "Two years and ten months." He buffed the display window of his calculator with a thumb.

"I like the shoes," Marci abruptly said.

Klinger demurred. "They won't take much of this weather," he moved his head at the raindrops teeming down the window, "but they fit. What I like is the coat," he added. "If I ever get warm again, this coat will keep me that way."

"Did you spend all forty bucks?"

"That plus another sixteen."

"Receipt?" She held out her hand.

Klinger fished it out of the inside breast pocket of the peacoat and gave it to her.

She accepted it, then turned her head toward her own door's window. A moment later she sighed, fogging the glass.

Klinger was about to say thanks, it's been like touching the stars, open the door, and walk into the rain against traffic and never see this woman again, when she turned and said, "How'd you like to make a thousand bucks?"

The cabbie looked up from his calculator, blinked at the windshield in front of him, and went back to his figures.

"Well?" Marci asked Klinger.

Klinger narrowed his eyes. "On top of expenses?"

Marci shook her head and smiled a little smile. "But of course."

"You have my attention," Klinger admitted.

"Back to Goodwill," she said. Before Klinger could object she added, speaking to the cabbie, "Wait here."

"You wait," the cabbie said, looking up from his calculator. "You think I'm born yesterday?" He pointed at the meter, whose LEDs now formed the figure $72.55.

"Oh," Marci said. "Of course." She produced her wallet and handed a hundred-dollar bill over the driver's shoulder. "We'll be back."

The cabbie stretched the C-note between his two hands, held it up against the light, and nodded. "I'll be right here."

The crescendo of insanity inside the Goodwill had increased and Marci was picky, so the second trip took forty-five minutes.

While she shopped for him, Klinger made a beeline for the dressing room in which he'd changed. It was unoccupied, but his wet clothes were gone. So much for the bindle of speedball.

When they got back in the cab Klinger was dressed in

a dark tweed jacket with black elbow patches, a pineapple shirt, dark slacks, the same shoes, and a plaid fedora with a little feather stuck in the band. He carried his earlier purchases in a large paper shopping bag.

Marci slid across the back seat until she was directly behind the driver. "That was fun," she told Klinger, as he followed her into the cab and out of the rain. "I haven't dressed a man since a fly-by-night liposuction clinic paralyzed my father."

Klinger had just settled into his seat. Hearing Marci's quip, he started to get out again.

"Hey." Marci laughed and put her hand on his arm. "Take it easy."

Klinger froze. "Taking it easy," he said to the rain, "has never gotten me anywhere."

"Did you keep the receipt?" she asked him.

Klinger sat back into the seat and closed the door against the rain. "No, darling," Klinger said faintly, "I think you have it."

She looked about her person, then plucked the corner of a white slip of paper out of the wad of cash in her hand. "Here it is." She folded the slip and tucked it into a zippered compartment of her chamois wallet, parallel to a neat sheaf of legal tender. "Service uniform." She dropped the wallet into her briefcase/purse. "A definite write-off," she noted contentedly.

"Speaking of which . . ." The cabbie touched the meter, whose LEDs now read $102.35.

"I'll need a receipt for that, too," Marci remarked. "When the time comes."

The cabbie retrieved three blank receipts from under the sun visor and handed them over his shoulder. "Where to now?"

"Look," Klinger said.

The cabbie changed his angle of sight so as to see Klinger.

"Yes?" Marci said.

"About this hole in my stomach?" Klinger placed the flat of his hand over the lower-left side of his belly. "I need to put something on it."

Marci consulted her phone. "It's past lunch time, it's true."

"I'd be willing to start with breakfast," Klinger said. "Then lunch."

"Okay," Marci said. "We'll start with your place across from the hospital." Marci watched Klinger as he closed his eyes, his hand still covering that part of his stomach. When he made no response she told the driver, "Pine and Hyde."

The cabbie watched his mirror. "You want I should wait again?"

Her thoughts clearly elsewhere, Marci shook her head vaguely.

"All good things must come to an end," the driver said. He pulled the machine into gear and studied its side-view mirror. When it became safe to merge into traffic he did so, asking the while, "Did anybody in this vehicle ever wonder how many Hummers it would take to equal the density of the neutron star that's at the heart of the Crab Nebula? No? Well, take heart. A Chinese-Iranian consortium has given considerable thought to the problem . . ."

With a generous tip, the cab fare added up to one hundred and sixty dollars. Once seated in the diner, Marci dutifully filled out all three of the business-card size receipts in order to reflect a total of twice that.

"Right off the top," she said to Klinger, as she filed the swatches of yellow pasteboard in the wallet compartment with the thrift-shop and other receipts.

They were in the same booth he and Frankie had occupied . . . had that been just yesterday? Klinger relaxed his aching frame against the cushions. "This grand you mentioned. Is that tax deductible, too?"

"One-time day labor subcontract," Marci replied without hesitation. "Absolutely deductible." She smiled sweetly. "I'll need your address and Social Security number."

Klinger's gut really was bothering him this morning. He closed his eyes a little too tightly. "Why's that?"

"So I can 1099 you."

A minute passed. "What kind of beef is that?"

Marci looked puzzled. "Beef?"

The waitress brought coffee. Klinger opened his eyes. It was the same waitress, too. She made no sign that she recognized him. Clothes make the man. Klinger watched her walk away. Had that really been just yesterday?

"Are you serious about that grand?" he asked abruptly.

Marci nodded.

"Okay." Klinger stood up. "I'll be right back." He walked out the front door, looked both ways, took a right and disappeared.

Marci watched him go. After a moment she shrugged, took out her phone, and applied her thumbs to it.

Upon his return Klinger sat back into the booth, made a couple of moves beneath the edge of the table, topped off his coffee from a half-pint of whiskey in a paper sack, recapped it, and dropped the package into the inside breast pocket of his new-to-him tweed jacket.

Marci raised a dubious eyebrow. "That ought to fix the hole in your stomach."

Klinger lifted the mug to his lips and sipped. "One man's ambrosia is another man's hotshot," he took a second sip, "is the primary tenet of Pragmatism." He drained half the cup and set it down again.

Marci, texting, nodded as if she'd understood every word.

The waitress appeared bearing sausage, eggs, grits, toast, butter, and jam, all for Klinger, and a cup of black tea with a bowl of oatmeal and blueberries for Marci.

"I suppose it could be both," Marci observed.

"Yeah," Klinger said, not bothering to conceal his uninterest in her opinion.

After he'd tucked away about two-thirds of his meal, Klinger slowed down enough to ask her why and what for.

Marci retrieved Phillip's phone from her purse and set it on the table. "Without a password, this phone is useless."

"The new battery isn't enough, huh?"

"The battery isn't enough."

Klinger caught the waitress's eye by raising his coffee cup. "And with a password?"

"Hard to say," Marci admitted. "But it's something we need to find out."

The waitress appeared with a pot of coffee. "Leave plenty of room for cream," Klinger requested. "So you can't just ask your buddy for the password?"

"He won't give it to me," Marci said. "But he might give it to you."

Klinger, about to redouble the dose of whiskey, thought better of it, capped the bottle, and handed it over the tabletop. "Would you mind putting this in your purse?"

Marci looked at the paper sack, then at Klinger.

Klinger waited.

She took the bottle and put it in her purse.

Klinger set about pursuing the balance of his meal. "So it's a con."

"Is that what you call it?"

"If the idea is for me to go into this guy's hospital room and con the password out of him—yes, I'd call it a con."

"I'm thinking that's the only way it's going to work," Marci confided.

Klinger crosscut a length of sausage and speared it with his fork. "Why shouldn't he give it up to you? He knows you, right? You're friends?"

Marci drew a little circle on the Formica with the tip of her forefinger. "Phillip," she sighed.

While Klinger waited, chewing, he idly wondered if her answer was going to be a lie because it needed to be a lie, or because she liked lying.

"Okay, okay," she said, as she self-consciously watched the forefinger. "Phillip knows that I know that he has another girlfriend, and he thinks that, while I have a pretty good idea, I'm not really positive who she is." She looked out the window next to them. "I mean, I can't prove who she is." She sighed, then looked at Klinger. "But if she's who I think she is, things are going to go very badly for Phillip and, not so incidentally, for me and for the company that Phillip and I both work for."

Klinger forked what was left of his grits into his mouth and laid his utensil across the empty plate. "Wait a minute." He dabbed his lips with his napkin. "You and this guy Phillip are an item? Phillip is your intended? Your fiancé? The guy for whom you'd like to gain some . . . experience?"

By way of an answer, she retrieved her own phone from her purse, swiped it five or six times, considered the result, swiped some more, then turned the screen so Klinger could see it.

"Wow," Klinger said after a moment. "She's almost as pretty as you are."

Marci blushed a deep crimson. "That's not a very good picture," she said. "She's a lot prettier than that."

"Does she always wear so little clothing?"

"It's a vacation photo," Marci said defensively. "She was in Hawaii."

"And might I ask how it came into your possession?"

Marci bit her lower lip.

"On the one hand, you don't have to tell me. On the other hand, I'm sure I'd never be able to guess, even if I wanted to." Klinger pointed at the screen. "On the third hand, do I need to know?"

Marci made the picture go away and placed the phone, screen down, on the table top. "One day at the office he went to lunch and left his e-mail open on his computer," she said simply. "I'm not proud of it." She tapped the phone with a fingernail. "But she's not after Phillip for his body." Her mouth tightened. "Or his mind, or his heart."

Klinger lifted his hands. "What else is there?"

Marci raised her eyes and looked at Klinger. "Computer programming."

"I might have known." Klinger shook his head. "Of course." He nodded. "How stupid of me."

"Work that Phillip has done," Marci continued in all seriousness. "And work that only he knows how to do. He's one of the best."

An image of Frankie Geeze flitted across Klinger's mind. Frankie Geeze had been a man whose work was unique and irreplaceable. Frankie Geeze had been one of the best.

The best weren't faring too well, of late.

"So this babe." Klinger pointed at the phone. "She's like a spy?"

Marci lowered her voice. "She's a double agent."

By now Klinger no longer believed a word Marci was saying.

"So she's like schtupping your buddy Phillip in the hope that he'll blurt a trade secret at the moment of ecstasy?"

"About five thousand lines of code," Marci said. "That's almost exactly it. A module of code, what they call an object. Anybody who writes an app—?"

"Oh, an app," Klinger shook his head.

Marci brightened. "You know from apps?"

Klinger held up a hand, its palm toward Marci, and definitely shook his head.

"Well," Marci said, "if you did? Phillip's object would make your life a lot easier."

"What's this chick's name?"

The merest quiver passed over Marci's lower lip. "Taffy Quesada."

Klinger frowned. "Outside of *chiva*, *adiós*, and *hombre de negocios*, I don't speak much Spanish," he said. "But is Taffy the feminine form?"

Marci took her turn at frowning. "What is *chiva*?"

"Heroin," Klinger told her simply.

Marci's mouth formed the word *oh*, but did not articulate it aloud. "Taffy," she said after a moment, "is—how shall I put it—is a very feminine form."

"I see. So is what this Taffy person doing illegal?"

"Yes." Marci shook her head glumly. "But if Phillip lets her get away with it, and by the time any resulting litigation could kick in?" She shook her head. "The industry will have moved on in the meantime and the question of legality will pretty much be moot."

Klinger's eyes hardened. "Like I got any fucking idea what you're talking about."

Marci nodded. She scratched the back of her phone with a fingernail, and she watched her fingernail as she did it. As the back of her phone was covered with scratches that ran parallel to the new ones, Klinger realized that this must be a habit of hers.

"Sometimes," she said, as if directing her reflections to

the back of her cellphone, "I think I'd be better off being more like you."

"Oh?" said Klinger. "And how's that?"

Marci shrugged. "A drunk who lives in a hotel when he has the money, and who knows absolutely nothing about cellphones, or intellectual property rights, or deception, betrayal, corporate espionage . . ." She looked up and flashed a sad smile. "Or women."

Klinger regarded her as if from a long distance and a long time away. If space, i.e. context, really told matter how to move, Klinger would have been long gone from the corner of Hyde and Pine. "I know everything I need to know about women," he finally said. "And nothing about computers."

Marci went from scratching the back of her cellphone to tapping it. "Doesn't make any difference," she said. She lifted her eyes. "You can always use a thousand bucks."

She assessed him frankly.

"Am I right?"

FIFTEEN

Room 833 was as far away from the elevator bank as a room could get, and it was private, as Klinger couldn't help but notice. He'd only ever been on hospital wards that consisted entirely of parallel rows of beds. When Klinger had been forced to spend a little time in hospital, privacy hadn't been an issue.

Klinger loosened his tie—yes, Marci had bought him a red tie, and a blue shirt to go underneath it.

"Don't tell me," he had told her, as they stood before the bank of elevators in the street-level lobby, "how long it's been since you've tied a man's tie."

"Since they paralyzed my father." She looked him in the eye, then looked back at the knot. "Except his, I tied real tight."

Klinger, who had never worn a tie in his life, jutted his chin to one side.

"Just remember," she whispered.

"A thousand bucks," he remembered.

She slipped the phone into the side pocket of his jacket. "The Gavel," she reminded him. "Cocktails at five o'clock." She winked. "On me."

Klinger walked down the hall, past the nurse's station, past an empty gurney, past a couple of televisions, and pushed open the door to 833.

Phillip couldn't have been thirty years old, but he looked older. The fluorescent lights didn't help, but his complexion was unnaturally wan, preternaturally sallow, and one big purpling where it wasn't a yellowing contusion. His left ear was twice the size of its mate and mostly bandaged. His exposed right arm had a couple of tubes leading to it, with bruises apposite to their needles. He wasn't breathing correctly, and he was being helped by a mask over his nose and mouth, a tube from which led to an erratically clicking machine on a stand next to the bed. A wire draped over his shoulder led to a dill-pickle-type call button parked on his chest. A TV remote lay on the bedclothes, but the television, which hung over the entrance door, was turned off.

Phillip's room was a corner unit, too, with not one but two windows. A ceiling-to-floor curtain hung from the bed's right side, apparently to shield the patient from the northern exposure which, despite rainwater coursing down the window, flooded the room with light.

It was two-thirty in the afternoon, and Phillip seemed to be sleeping.

As he waited for Phillip's subconscious to notice his presence, Klinger took in the details of the room. A chair, upholstered in slick green Naugahyde, stood to the bed's right, Klinger's left. On one wall hung a picture of the Transamerica Pyramid. There was a door, presumably to a bathroom, in the wall to the left of the bed. The slide track for the curtain entirely circled the bed, but only the curtain to its right had been deployed. The headboard of the bed had been cranked up so that the patient assumed a half-sitting posture. The usual clipboard hung from a hook on the foot of the bed. Several magazines devoted to the exigencies of celebrity culture lay atop a bedside stand, along with a thermometer bottle, a couple of brown prescription pill bottles, a clock radio, a nail clipper, a comb, a box of disposable tissues. Next to the little night table were a stainless steel tree hung with dripbags and next to that a roll-around rack of electronic gear.

Klinger had a look at the labels on the pill bottles. The first contained an antibiotic. The second label mentioned thirty forty-milligram ampules of a brand-name synthesis of opium-derived thebaine.

These latter pills would bring thirty-five dollars apiece on the street. Without so much as a backward glance, Klinger cracked the cap, dispensed four ampules into the palm of his hand, dropped them into his shirt pocket, replaced the cap on the bottle and the bottle onto the nightstand, and was standing at the foot of the bed, retrieving the phone from his jacket pocket, when a nurse stuck his head in the door.

"Did you say your name was Officer Clemens?" he asked.

As if holding the phone away from the north light in order to study its screen, Klinger didn't bother to turn to face the nurse. "Is Clemens on this case too?"

"In other words," the nurse said, as if annoyed with the obtuse answer and the wasted moment that went with it, "you're not him."

Tentatively touching the phone, Klinger gave it a moment before he shook his head. "No. I'm not him."

"Shit," the nurse said, and went on his away.

The door to the hall closed silently.

"This is the longest," a muffled voice said, "that I've gone without e-mail in my adult life."

Klinger looked up. The patient's eyes were open, and he was looking hungrily at the phone in Klinger's hand. "Somebody took my phone," Phillip said.

"Good afternoon," Klinger said. "Phillip Wong, I presume?"

"It is I," Phillip Wong replied. "Or what's left of me. Phoneless and e-mailless me." Phillip looked at Klinger, frowned uncertainly, looked at the red tie, shook off the thought and asked, "And whom do I address?"

Well, thought Klinger, you almost remembered me. "Detective Schnorr," Klinger said without hesitation. "SFPD."

"The police?"

Klinger nodded. "The police. And how are you feeling, Mr. Wong?—May I call you Phillip?"

"Of course."

"Thanks. Call me Reese."

"What day is it, Reese?"

"Friday," Klinger answered. "All day."

"And how long have I been here?"

Klinger considered this. "Eighteen hours, maybe?"

"I got a headache."

"I'll bet." Klinger took up the clipboard and had a look. Much of the language and notation were opaque to him, but he knew what a concussion was. "You took quite a whack."

Phillip tried to nod, but he winced instead. "I don't remember a thing."

"What's the last thing you do remember?" Klinger lifted the first page off the clipboard.

Though it no doubt hurt, Phillip's expression soured. "Marci," he said bitterly. "Fucking Marci on the fucking phone."

Klinger looked up from the clipboard. "And Marci is …?"

Phillip sighed. "An associate." His sigh made a lot of noise inflating his ventilator. "An associate from my job."

"I see." Klinger replaced the clipboard on its hook. "Do you remember where you were, or what you were doing, while you were talking to her?"

"Sure," Phillip said. "I was eating pasta and drinking wine at the … At the …"

"You had dinner in a place called Il Bodega di Frisco," Klinger told him. "Is that when you talked to her?"

"That's right," Phillip said. "I love that place. There's never anybody there."

"Interesting," Klinger lied. "I wonder how they stay in business?"

"They run a sports book out back," Phillip said off-handedly. "I—." He shut up.

Klinger nodded a jaded nod. "We know all about the sports book."

When Phillip's eyes widened, the disparity in pupil size became obvious. "How come you—?"

"Are you kidding? If we took down all the gambling in North Beach, there wouldn't be a joint up there left to eat in. Not to mention to drink in." Klinger put one of his desert boots up on the railing at the foot of the bed and rezipped it. "What I really want to know is, how's the food at Il Bodega di Frisco?"

"After a week of eating sandwiches at your desk three times a day," Phillip said, "it's goddamn excellent. Especially the wine. They got a deep cellar under there somewhere." He squinted. "You ever eat sandwiches three meals a day?"

"Sure," Klinger said. "All the time. I never drink wine, though," he added truthfully. He placed the palm of his right hand over the lower-left side of his stomach. "It aggravates my digestion. But I drink a lotta coffee. Coffee and hot pastrami with the works—pickles, pepperoncini, onions, lettuce, mayo, mustard—." Klinger smiled contentedly. He sounded just like a cop. "What else?"

"Sprouts," Phillip suggested. "Avocado."

"Although sometimes," Klinger confided, "I go for a giro."

"I can't handle lamb." Phillip made a face. "Too greasy."

"You drink enough coffee?" Klinger dropped his foot back to the floor and chopped the side of one hand against the palm of its opposite. "Cuts right through the grease. I don't care what you've been eating."

Phillip groaned.

Five seconds passed in silence.

"I think I'm gonna puke," Phillip said.

Uh oh, Klinger thought. Aloud he said, "You want a wastebasket?"

Phillip smacked his lips and moved his head back and forth.

"No good if you puke inside that mask," Klinger submitted nervously. "Maybe I'll get a nurse," he lied.

Phillip held out a hand. "Give me a minute," he managed to say. "Give me . . ."

Klinger gave him two. In the intervening silence, while keeping one eye on the patient, Klinger paced the room. On the cover of a celebrity magazine a former governor of Alaska was astride an ATV and showing a lot of leg. Out the north-facing window, despite the mist, he could make out the top of the south tower of the Golden Gate Bridge.

The crisis passed. "Okay," said Phillip weakly. "I'm okay."

"How about some water?" asked Klinger.

Phillip nodded.

Klinger took up a plastic flask from the bedside stand. A glass tube protruded from its mouth, and the tube had a dogleg in it. "Is this water?"

Phillip nodded. Klinger held the flask in one hand and aimed the tube at Phillip's head with the other.

Phillip pressed the mask to his face, took several deep breaths, then moved the mask aside. Klinger quickly fit the end of the glass straw tube to Phillip's lips, and Phillip drew a long draught through it.

Nodding, Phillip pushed the straw aside, refit the mask over his nose and mouth, pressed it into place with palm of one hand, and inhaled greedily enough to con cave the transparent contours of the mask. The machine to which the mask was hooked ticked determinedly. Then Phillip exhaled loudly, as if exhausted. Beads of moisture flecked the inside surface of the mask. "Thanks," he managed to say.

Klinger replaced the flask on the table, then indicated the upholstered chair. "May I?"

Phillip nodded eagerly.

Klinger took a seat, retrieving the phone from his jacket pocket as he did so.

"You're racked up and you need your rest, Phillip. I won't keep you much longer. Is this your phone?"

Phillip's eyes brightened. "Sure looks like it."

"Is there some way you can tell for sure?"

Phillip nodded so that the tubes festooning him rattled. "How?"

Klinger handed him the phone. Phillip held the phone, swiped a finger over its screen, then again, then again. He looked happy. The transformation was something to see. "I'm surprised it's not dead," he said, watching the screen. "Did you charge it?"

"It was dead when we found it," Klinger said easily. "A guy in the precinct has the same model. He loaned me— you—a battery."

Phillip nodded. "Where'd you find it?"

"Well get to that in a minute. It's password protected," Klinger added.

Phillip nodded again.

"The thing is," Klinger continued, "there's a chance the guy who mugged you made a few calls after he stole it. He might have been that stupid, anyway. That's if you'd left it on when he stole it, of course."

"I can check that," Phillip said. "Easily."

"Yeah," Klinger said. "I'm sure you can."

"Here we go," Phillip said. As Klinger watched, Phillip held the phone in front of him in his left hand, then, despite the resistance of the various tubes inhibiting his agility, placed the first three fingers of his right hand across the face of it. The phone emitted three escalating tones.

"Wow," Klinger repeated truthfully.

"It's my phone all right," Phillip said.

"Your password has to do with fingerprint recognition?" Klinger realized, amazed.

"Three-fingerprint recognition," Phillip nodded. "It's an open source app that I modified," he added modestly.

"Wow," Klinger replied frankly.

Phillip tapped the screen, waited, tapped again, waited, and tapped again. "Okay," he said. "Here's the call I took from Marci. Initiated at 8:37 p.m., terminated at 9:05 p.m. Pretty much the whole time I was trying to enjoy my meal."

"Marci's the associate you mentioned?" said Klinger.

Phillip nodded. "But I see no other incoming calls, and no outgoing calls. Not that night, anyway. But," he added, "there's . . . eleven incoming calls that went to my InBox starting at . . . one-thirty the next morning."

"Can you tell who they were from?"

Phillip nodded. "Marci . . . Marci . . . Then, yesterday, all kinds of people . . ." He tapped the side of the phone. "Then, this morning, Marci again." Phillip Wong sighed. "All work-related. Speaking clinically," he added, "I don't have too many friends."

Klinger pursed his lips. "Okay. But he still had the phone on him."

Phillip didn't look up from his screen. "Who did?"

"The guy we arrested this morning for . . ." Klinger hesitated.

Phillip waited a few seconds, then, his forefinger in midswipe, he looked at Klinger. "For?"

". . . Driving a stolen vehicle," Klinger decided. He shrugged. "It was a complete fluke. A coincidence." He nodded. "Guy has a long record, this is a high-end phone, and he had a cheap one in his possession that seemed way more obviously his speed. One of those pay-as-you-go phones you get out of a vending machine."

Phillip made a face.

"Also," Klinger went on, "he was in possession of several freshly dispensed ATM twenties whose serial numbers," he pointed at Phillip, "we traced to the North Beach branch of your bank."

"You know," Phillip frowned, "I vaguely remember using an ATM recently . . ."

"And so you did," Klinger nodded. "At something like ten-forty the night you got mugged. So," he indicated the phone, "our boy was driving a stolen car and in possession of stolen property. Too bad about the outgoing calls, though. If he'd been dumb enough to call his mother on your phone, it would be pretty easy to stick him with a couple of extra charges, and felonies at that."

"Like what felonies?"

"The stolen vehicle's a good one. And your ATM money. The phone was stolen too—right?"

"Right," Phillip nodded gravely. "Definitely."

"Okay," Klinger put out his hand. "Would you mind giving it back to me?"

Phillip look distressed. He looked at Klinger, then he looked at his phone. "But you just returned it to me," he said defensively. "What do you need it for?"

"It's evidence," Klinger said.

"Evidence . . ." Phillip said uncertainly. "But . . . But it's my phone." He gestured with it. "I got to return all these calls. All my numbers are in here. My address book. E-mail. I—."

Klinger nodded as if patiently. "I understand that, Phillip. Really, I do." Klinger patted the breast pocket of his jacket. "If I lost my phone, I'd be fucked. My whole case load would fall apart."

"Well?" Phillip replied. "You're making my point for me."

"Yes, yes," Klinger nodded. "But—."

Again, Phillip made as if to object, and, in doing so, he held the phone away from Klinger. Phillip's intravenous tubes moved with his right arm, and the IV tree, being on wheels, rolled into the curtain.

Klinger caught the IV tree with one hand and held his other hand aloft, its palm toward the patient. "Wait, Phillip, don't get excited. I'm not saying you're not going to get your phone back. What I'm saying, however, is that your phone is evidence collected in the course of an investigation. At the very least we need—."

"Creation of Tron," by Wendy Carlos, woke up Phillip's phone.

"Whoa," Klinger said. As Phillip made to answer the call, Klinger held out a hand. "Wait."

Phillip blinked. The ringtone repeated.

"Do you recognize the incoming number?" Klinger asked.

Phillip stared at him, blinked, then looked at the screen. The ringtone repeated a third time. "No," he said.

"It'll stay in memory," Klinger said, "right?"

Phillip nodded.

"You want me to answer it?" Klinger said.

Phillip, as if entranced by the screen, ignored him.

Klinger put his hand on Phillip's shoulder. "At least put it on speaker."

Phillip blinked, then nodded. He touched the screen once, nodded, then touched it again. "Hello?" he said, holding the phone equidistant between Klinger's head and his own.

"Marty?" a woman's voice said.

"Who?" Phillip said. "I mean," he corrected himself, noticing Klinger's visible wince, "Hello? Yes?"

"Who is this?" said the little speaker. The voice was muffled and there was a lot of noise in the background. It sounded like freeway traffic and maybe even a helicopter.

"Hello?" Phillip repeated.

The caller rang off.

"You don't know the number—right?"

Phillip shook his head.

"And the voice?"

"No," Phillip said.

Klinger retrieved a pen and a little spiral notebook from the breast pocket of his jacket. "What's the number?"

Phillip read it aloud. Klinger wrote it down. "Let me ask you something."

"Sure."

"If somebody found this phone, or stole it, is there a way for them to figure out the number that rings it?"

Phillip smiled. "I think so." He turned the phone edgewise and showed it to Klinger. There, as Klinger could see, a ten-digit number was etched into the edge of the phone.

"That's the number?" Klinger asked in amazement.

"I can recite a hundred lines of assembler instructions without making a mistake," Phillip said shyly. "But I've never been able to remember my own phone number. Besides," he added, "until very recently, if you changed phone companies or even plans within a company, you had to change phone numbers, too. I've had a million phones and almost as many phone numbers and plans to go with them. Oh yes," Phillip nodded his head gravely, "I go all the way back."

Klinger raised both eyebrows, nonplussed.

Phillip brooded a moment. "Sometimes I think the modern world just asks too much of its citizens." He looked at Klinger. Above the seams of the ventilator mask, the unequal sizes of Phillip's pupils clearly indicated a concussion. "Don't you?"

"Sure, kid," Klinger said. After a pause, he resumed copying the phone's number into his notebook. "Unlike the clowns in the police department, I'll bet this clown we caught noticed this number here and passed it on to his girlfriend or his mother. We missed that detail entirely. But if we could make that connection, we'd have a pretty airtight case. Tell you what, Phillip. Let me borrow your phone long enough to run it by our technical people again. Maybe they can trace that incoming call. I'll bring it back tomorrow, about this time, I promise." Klinger replaced pen and notebook into his jacket pocket. "You think you can be a phoneless citizen of this crazy world for another twenty-four hours?" He favored Phillip with a warm smile. "I'm sure you can use the rest. A concussion is no joke. I know." Klinger tapped the side of his head.

Phillip looked just a little lost, and then he looked just a little chagrined. "Sure, Officer." He handed Klinger the phone. "I've enjoyed my semi-conscious morning on drugs and without a phone. I guess I never realized how demanding a phone can be."

"I appreciate the trust," Klinger said sincerely, accepting the phone. "I need one more favor."

Phillip knitted his fingers together, folded his hands over his chest, and gazed dreamily at the ceiling. "Name it."

"I need you to override your password on this thing, just long enough for the lab boys to check it out thoroughly. Don't worry," Klinger added, "they won't be calling your girlfriends or anything like that."

"Girlfriends?" Phillip said sourly. He took back the phone. "No problem." He manipulated the phone with multiple touches and swipes, powered it down, counted to ten, powered it back up again, tested it to his satisfaction, powered it down again, and handed the device back to Klinger. "Now you've got access to anything on it."

Klinger looked at it. "Even if the battery dies?"

"Even then. Even if it goes to sleep," Phillip said drowsily. "No password required. Just . . . fire it . . ." Phillip's eyes almost closed, then he opened them. "If you find any girlfriends in there, bookmark them for me."

He closed his eyes again.

"Thanks, guy," Klinger said. "If the lab boys get done with it by tonight, I'll drop it off on my way home, after my shift."

"Keep the son . . . of . . . a . . . a bitch . . ." Phillip said, not bothering to try keeping his eyes open.

Alone in the elevator, its doors closed and going down, Klinger sagged backward into a corner and closed his eyes. The car shuddered the eight stories down the shaft without making another stop, and Klinger was grateful for that. As the doors opened onto the lobby, he pulled himself together. People flooded past him, looking to go up.

As he made his way toward the street exit, Klinger thought that this must have been the longest short con he'd ever undertaken. Unless you counted his life. Either way, the strain had wrung him out, and he needed a drink.

Pondering the difference he missed the chance to exit the revolving door, and had to go around again.

S I X T E E N

In the appointed cocktail lounge, a dark-curtained joint called the Gavel two blocks west of the Federal Court Building, Antonio Carlos Jobim drifted along deep pile carpet and mahogany wainscoting and big-shouldered chandeliers and subdued chatter of a thinning crowd lingering over coffee and digestifs as its participants decided whether or not to go back to work or call it a weekend.

It's Friday, one of them reminded his companions, as Klinger passed their table on the way to the bar, what the heck, either they're out on bail or they have a dry place to sleep until Tuesday. Agreeable laughter. Another round? No thanks, I'm going to the gym later. And what about you? Sure: I'm going to hell any time now. Agreeable laughter . . .

It was ten minutes after five. He didn't see her at a table, nor was she in the bar, at which he reluctantly took a stool. The bartender, who wore black slacks, and an open-necked white shirt, a black vest and black sleeve garters, placed a coaster in front of Klinger that advertised a single-malt Scotch at twenty-five dollars a pop. He ordered his usual, double and on the rocks.

A copy of the *Wall Street Journal* lay on the bar, and just as Klinger was thinking he was going to have to begin to read it, Phillip Wong's phone went off in his pocket.

He might have heard that ringtone a thousand times and not known it for the obscure piece of music it was. He slapped the pocket like it contained a live snake.

It went off a second time, louder than the first, before

he retrieved it and, imitating billions of other people, he held the thing next to his face and told it hello.

"You have it," she said.

"I have it," he agreed.

"You're in the Gavel?"

"I'm in the Gavel."

"I'll be there in two shakes of a lamb's tail."

Klinger frowned. "Are you in a laundromat?"

After but a moment's hesitation, she laughed. "How did you know?"

"That noise in the background? It sounds like sneakers in a dryer."

She lowered her voice. "A guy who just loaded a pair of sneakers into a dryer down the line from the change machine, here, didn't want to put his blanket in there with them." After a moment she added, "He's sitting in a roll-around basket in front of his dryer, watching it go round and round, while he holds his blanket and sucks his thumb."

The bartender placed a rocks glass containing a single ice cube and an inch and a half of whiskey on the coaster in front of Klinger, put a check face down beside it, and went away without a word.

"I think I know that guy," Klinger said. He turned up a corner of the check as if it were a hole card, just enough to read the amount. Eighteen dollars plus tax—a dollar seventy-six—might as well add up to twenty, even if he were to stiff the bartender his tip. He smoothed and resmoothed the face-down check with the side of his hand as if he were considering a bluff. The check's a double, the drink's a single, the guy's stiffing me, and I'm going to stiff him. Now there's a social contract.

"So now you're doing laundry?"

She laughed easily. "I could have been doing your laundry."

Klinger could hardly believe what he was hearing. He shook his head. "Look—," he began.

"What it is," she interrupted, "is, these places always have change machines, and I always need change for parking. So," her shrug came right down the line, "I ducked in for a short transaction."

Just show up with my grand, Klinger said to himself. Just show up and trade my grand for this telephone and let's go our separate ways. And—"Forget my laundry," he said aloud.

"Plus," she added meaningfully, "This place is dry and it's right next to an ATM."

Klinger didn't raise his voice. "So we're meeting any time now," he said tightly. "Right?" He siphoned a little whiskey. "I can't afford to be lingering in this luxe clipjoint."

"I'm on the way." She hung up.

Klinger looked at the screen on the phone. DISCONNECT? it asked him. WARNING, the screen added, DEVICE UNLOCKED. Klinger narrowed his eyes. It seemed to him he remembered something about these things. He touched the disconnect query and held his finger there. The phone disconnected, lingered as if thinking about it, then a new message appeared: SHUT DOWN? Klinger fingered YES. The phone shut down.

Thank fucking god, he sighed raggedly. He pocketed the phone and devoted his attention to his drink.

By the time Marci arrived, twenty minutes later, Klinger had finished his first double and ordered a second—so he was down forty bucks already. But hey, he admonished the amber cylinder of his cocktail, glistening as if impatiently before him, you gotta spend money to make money.

This thought, however, did not delude him into playing the high roller. When the bartender, no doubt suspicious of Klinger's overall solvency, asked him to square up,

Klinger peeled off a couple of twenties, told him to keep the change, and let his eyes say it all: Keep the forty-eight cents, you fucking cunt, and take it to the Kentucky Derby.

That's the hieratic attitude, he assured himself: blame the help.

She placed the shopping bag full of warm clothing on the floor between stools, draped her raincoat atop her purse/briefcase and the furled brolly atop it all, and assumed the stool to Klinger's left.

Noting the uptick in customer quality, the bartender dealt her a coaster right away, as if from a deck of them he kept in a universe parallel to the one in which he kept the deck from which he dealt to the likes of Klinger. "Cappuccino," she told him. "I'm still on the clock," she added modestly.

The perky insouciance of this stipulation rubbed Klinger entirely the wrong way. She was on the clock? His hands on the rail in front of him, the one removed from the drink just to give it something to do until the time came to refresh the palate, clenched. You're on the clock? he said to the eight inches of bar rail between the hands. *I'm always on the clock.*

"Everything go smoothly?" she asked.

Klinger wagged a finger.

She frowned.

"The bottle," he said quietly.

Her mouth formed the syllable *Oh* without uttering it. She plucked the brown paper sack from her purse and handed it over. Klinger had it uncapped, his drink topped off, the jug recapped, and the bag in the side pocket of his jacket before the bartender had properly tamped the grounds in the basket strainer.

"How's Phillip?"

"Pretty racked up, by the look of him," Klinger said weakly.

"He's going to live—right?"

"Do you care?"

Marci took great umbrage at this remark. "Care?" she admonished him. "Of course I care. I've known Phillip since . . . Since . . . We've been . . . We were . . ."

Klinger cut it short. "He's going to be fine." He put the phone on the bar.

She looked at it.

"Go ahead," Klinger said, taking up his drink with both hands. "Make a call."

She touched the phone. The screen flickered to life.

"Careful," Klinger said. "It's got a hell of a ringtone."

Marci laughed nervously, then nodded. "It's from Phillip's favorite movie. I forget the name of it."

"Is there some way to make it go away?"

The bartender appeared with a foaming cappuccino, set it on the bar in front of Marci, landed a little bowl of sugar cubes, both brown and white, interleaved with various packets of artificial sweetener, pink, white, and blue, and went away.

"It's loud and nerve-racking," Klinger added.

Marci nodded. "If it weren't annoying, you wouldn't pay any attention to it," she commented absently. She took a sip of her coffee with one hand and fingered the screen of Phillip's phone with the other.

"Hey."

She set down her cup, but didn't divert her attention from the phone.

"Hey," Klinger repeated.

She looked up midswipe. "Oh." Her attention reverted to the phone. "Hand me my purse."

Klinger retrieved the briefcase/purse from beneath the raincoat and handed it to her.

Still with one hand on the phone, Marci unzipped the

mouth of her purse, removed the chamois wallet, plucked a thickness of hundred-dollar bills from it, and slipped it into the side pocket of Klinger's jacket. "Pretend it's a banana-flavored condom," she whispered, and patted the pocket.

"What," Klinger said, frowning, "am I getting wood?"

"If I were a man," Marci cooed at the phone, "money would give me wood."

"You're not a man," Klinger watched her, "and money still gives you wood."

"True," she nodded. And, "Aha."

"Aha?"

She nodded happily.

"His e-mail password is entered automatically by his browser," she declared with a lilt.

"So a girl could effortlessly access a boy's e-mail," Klinger concluded, "if a girl were so minded to do."

"True enough. Not to mention a boy's cloud." Marci frowned. "Of course, he's got a lot of e-mail, and his cloud is big."

"Any from the girlfriend?" *Cloud* meant nothing to Klinger and, despite the compelling nature of the conversation, his mind had begun to tilt along toward its conception of his future. A slightly better hotel room, a tub full of scalding hot water, with epsom salts and scented bath oil, a fifth of whiskey, a bucket of ice, a rocks glass instead of a plastic cup . . . The thought of epsom salts reminded him of Mary Fiducione. He could take the bath at her place and buy her dinner for once.

"Girlfriend?" Marci said, not really paying attention.

"Yeah," Klinger said, not really paying attention either.

"Oh," Marci said, abruptly recollecting herself. "She's probably in here somewhere . . ." But her attention was elsewhere.

"Uh huh," Klinger agreed without conviction.

"Let's query 'me,'" Marci suggested half aloud.

"Let's do that," Klinger said, evincing no interest whatsoever. The bartender floated by long enough to deposit a receipt in a tray in front of Klinger, with one quarter, two dimes, and three pennies atop it, and another check, face down, in front of Marci's cappuccino.

"And there it is," Marci said happily to the phone. "Zipped under its proper name, yet."

"Which would be?"

"Object_10," she told the phone, "dot zip."

Dot zip, Klinger repeated to himself. Banana-flavored object ten dot zip equals one thousand bucks. He sipped his drink and set down the glass. He carefully centered the glass on its coaster with both hands. He fell to wondering if and when he had ever had a thousand dollars in his pocket.

"I think the FTP site would be a good place to park it," Marci said to the phone. "Give it its own folder . . . Maybe a subfolder? Change the name while we're about it. We need a mnemonic so we can remember what the hell we're doing . . ."

There had been that caper involving a forty-foot trailer full of stainless steel motorcycle footpegs, Klinger was thinking, in San Luis Obispo. But that had been a thousand dollars total, which he'd had to split with two other guys. Both of whom went to prison, as he had to remind himself. In order to spare the county the expense of a trial, there had been a deal. One guy took the grand larceny rap, the other stood still for a parole violation, convicted felon in possession of narcotics, though he had to go back to school and do at least another nickel for it. Better than another strike, though. And Klinger's name got left out of it. He moved into a cabin with a kitchenette behind a truck stop in King City, where the three hundred and thirty-three dollars lasted him a month. That had been . . . He exercised his mind as regards the subject, but to little avail. Quite a long time ago, he decided. For that matter, he realized, and if so, both of those guys should have gotten out by now. One of them, at least. What was his name, anyway? Alfredo, the parole violator, Alfredo Potrero, had been pretty advanced in age. Could he have outlived his sentence?

"Done," Marci said. She offered the phone to Klinger. "Want to make a call?"

Klinger looked at the phone, then looked at Marci. "No, thanks." He shook his head. "I don't know anybody with a phone."

"Surely there's somebody," Marci cajoled. "How about your mother?"

Klinger failed to see the humor.

"Oh," Marci said. "Sorry." She powered down the cellphone.

"We're done, too," Klinger said. "Right?"

She stared at him for a moment. Then her lips parted slightly, as if she were about to say something, then she appeared to reconsider, and they closed again. "Right," she said softly. She nodded and added, "Right . . ." She reached for her wallet.

Klinger, who had turned back to his drink, lifted his glass to his lips and paused to say, "I'll get that."

She hesitated.

"Girlfriend, my ass," Klinger said over the rim of his glass. The mirror behind a row of single-malt Scotches, ranged above the back bar countertop, reflected her profile.

Without another word, Marci stood off her stool. When she'd gathered her things she said softly, "I'm very grateful for your help."

A certain rigidity had entered Klinger's physique, a stiffening due to the damp, the cold—and the resentment, it seemed, or some kind of residual unrecognized feedback that pissed him off. But hey, he admonished himself, what business is it of mine? So what if I have no idea what this seemingly straight, innocent, scheming, ambitious, and ostensibly shallow chick is really up to, with that phone and her boyfriend or ex-boyfriend or fiancé and nonexistent other woman and, for that matter, with you, Klinger, yourself? Think of the contrast. Pretty ballsy, when you come to consider it. This little girl from another world drops in on Klinger, gets what she needs and ornithopters out again. He could practically hear the carbon fiber blades as they beat the moisture-saturated air. Though it would be more realistic, he considered, to be hearing the hiss of tires on an otherwise silent hybrid taxicab, as it chauffeured her out of his life forever.

Yes . . . She dropped in on his world, got what she needed, and moved on, up, out. Up, the key vector. Klinger, left to his own devices, and despite a thousand bucks cash in his pocket, would likely move down, and that sooner than later. Likely? Hah: certainly. Down was Klinger's totemic if dimensionless vector. Down was his destiny. Down was his color. Down was his town.

By the time Klinger returned his drink to its coaster, only ice remained in the glass and the woman Marci was gone.

Good riddance. He turned over her check. The cappuccino in this joint cost nine dollars, too.

Klinger stood off the barstool and reached into the front pocket of his trousers to retrieve what was left of his modest roll. He stopped. What am I doing, he said to himself. Just a little bit upstairs and a pace aft, I got a grand in C-notes. He retrieved his hand empty and rerouted it to the side pocket of his jacket. Where Klinger was going it would be good to have at least one of them broken. Where Klinger was going, while change for a hundred might be hard to come by, even regarded with suspicion, a hundred broken down to its constituent twenties would do for several evenings' entertainment.

And it wasn't until just about that very moment, as he peeled a bill away from its nine crisply folded brothers, that Klinger realized that, though he hadn't had a bank account in many, many years, there was one thing that he was pretty sure of, which was, automatic teller machines did not dispense hundred-dollar bills. Not yet, anyway. If they did, people would rob them more often.

Was that what had been bothering him?

He attracted the attention of the bartender, who took Marci's check and the hundred without so much as a wince. While he was away Klinger leaned on the bar, mulling things over. When the bartender returned, he counted ninety-one dollars into a tray and topped it off with the receipt for the nine-dollar cappuccino. The receipt now exhibited a single tear—paid. Conspicuously, the change included four twenties, a five, and six dollars in singles. No chump, our bartender. There's always the possibility of a tip, even from a sullen party in damp tweed.

Klinger retrieved every bill except one, a single, which he left on the tray, along with the receipt. Now you got a buck forty-eight to squander on the ponies, sport.

Always room for another one, though, he reminded himself thoughtfully, as he took up the damp if commodious thrift-shop shopping bag that contained his new-to-him pea coat and watch cap and trousers, now lofting the musk peculiar to damp wool.

He pushed out through the revolving door of the Gavel, where the storm raged unabated.

Hope your horse runs good in the rain, sport, he muttered to himself as he turned up the collar of his tweed jacket.

Always room for another sport, he reflected somewhat wryly, altogether damply, as he plunged into the downpour.

Always room for another sport. Especially in the great outdoors.

SEVENTEEN

Physically speaking, it's not all that far from the Gavel to the Hawse Hole; sociologically speaking, it's like jumping off a cliff. Weatherwise, on that particular Friday afternoon, it was like jumping off a cliff into the ocean.

Down through the streets he plummeted, shedding institutions, mores, raindrops, and dry cleaning fluid as he splashed puddle to puddle, waded over backed-up storm drains and flooded crosswalks, retaining only a sack of clothes, his memories, and a thousand bucks.

By the time he arrived at The Hawse Hole, Klinger was ready for a drink, he was ready to forget the last few days, he was ready for a change of clothing—Klinger was ready for anything but the future. Or the past. Or, as it turned out, the present.

By now it was six forty-five in the evening and, the sky being entirely packed with rain-bearing clouds, darkness was closing in. The blue neon chain that lowered itself, link by link, from the blue neon hawse hole high above the front door of the bar made a little splash of blue neon ploods, as it hit and lit the red neon anchor, just above the sidewalk, when all went blank until the chain lowered itself, link by link, again. As neon signs go, it was sufficiently boring to entice and encourage patrons to enter the bar simply to get away from it. Yes, though encased entirely in lexan long since, that the sign had outlasted the various milieus of the neighborhood, including its seafaring one, its lingering reputation as a good place to get shanghaied was something of a marvel. For that matter, the place was full of people who'd like nothing better than to get shanghaied. They'd perhaps come from all over the world hoping for the experience, only to find that the only ships docking in San Francisco these days needed skilled crew, crew who could teach scuba diving, for example, by day, while essaying bodacious karaoke by night, or lecture convincingly on currency markets as investment opportunities . . .

But still, as goes the no-frills *deus ex machina* romantic experience, the shanghai is hard to top.

Bruce was behind the plank, wearing denim instead of chaps, so perhaps St. Patrick's Day was over. Or, as Klinger shuddered to speculate, perhaps Bruce was sufficiently embarrassed at the damage done to cover it up.

The old man was there, too, and he was editorializing without an audience.

"The thing about life is this," he was saying, with barely a nod to Klinger, who, after dropping his nearly dissolved shopping bag under the bar sat four stools away from him. The old man held his hands aloft, palms some eighteen inches apart and cupped, each toward the other. "Life is a tunnel, see." He vibrated the two hands.

Klinger, staring at the empty bar top in front of him while marveling at how much water was dripping off him onto the floor, waited.

"You might have something there," Bruce said to a sheaf of twenties. But his tone was asking the old man whether he was done yet.

"Almost," the old man tossed off in Bruce's direction, as if telepathic. He continued to hold his hands in front of his face, some eighteen inches apart, with their palms cupped toward one another. "A continuum, like a tunnel," he repeated. "As a man moves through this tunnel of life, like it or not, he gives off vibrations." He wiggled his fingers.

"And the walls of the tunnel, which are composed of other people, absorb these vibrations."

Now Bruce forgot about his sheaf of twenties, and the ledger into which he was tabulating them, and turned to look at the old man.

Fingers still waggling, the old man moved his hands back and forth in the air in front of him, as if pumping a bellows. "The people impinged by your vibrations are your friends, your neighbors, family, acquaintances and business associates, even the people next to you on the bus who notice that you haven't bathed lately."

Klinger, who couldn't move on his stool without making squishing sounds, considered the irony of this.

"The sumtotal of the feedback from these entities constitutes the only reason to be reassured of your own existence. And, insofar as this continuum or tunnel that we call life may be sentient, it only stands to reason to think that it thinks that you exist, too." The old man clapped his hands once. "Astrology in a nutshell."

The street door opened. Two guys in flannel shirts entered, accompanied by the hiss of passing tires on the wet street. The door closed and the two new customers headed for the dogleg in the bar, six or eight stools into the gloom beyond the old man.

"When you die—," the old man cast his fingertips away from his face, "—your vibrations cease. The walls of the tunnel, however," he resumed wiggling his fingers, "continue as the media for your vibrations, which they propagate into the future despite your demise."

The two guys down the bar signaled Bruce. Bruce nodded his head, lifted a finger, and indicated the old man, conveying that he'd be along when the old man had finished. The two men looked from Bruce to the old man as if puzzled.

"The walls of the tunnel, however, are organic. That is to say, they consist entirely of a kind of deliquescing coherence. People are the sole medium of their and your own existence. None else can know you, and you can know no other. The Bible says so. Okay, the Bible doesn't say so. But, like you, people are organic and finite. People are born, they live, they die. Other shit happens to them. New experiences crowd out the old. Specifically, their memory of you fades. Some of them die off and, with them, their memories of everything, yourself included. It's bad enough that, with the expiration of one or another of them, that clean execution of that lugubrious Chopin Prelude winks out. But, never fear, another pianist will come along. You, on the other hand, are another matter. Only you can perform you. In other words, your vibrations are damped." The old man lowered his hands. "And so, it's precisely by means of the people you affected while you were alive that your memory lives on. So long as one of them lives, so you, too, will live. But after they've all died, after every single person that actually knew you is history, why, so then you too will have become history. And even if you are part of what the future calls history, your story will change. Alive people will remember an alive you. Once all of those who knew you are gone—in other words, once all the vibrations have been completely damped by their passage through the medium that is the walls of the tunnel of life—you will have truly ceased to exist. Which is why I predict that, even if the city fathers do cause Third Street to be renamed Willie E. Brown, Jr. Boulevard, it won't be too damn long before it's just another name for another street, and every bit as innocuous as the number three used to be. No more and no less. A street people will refer to by name, with no personality associated with it whatsoever. A dead end. Do you remember somebody called Polk? Or Fillmore? Or Hayes?

Who the hell was Brannan? Or Bryant? A *noumenon*—an object perceived by the communal intellect, and not by the senses. In other words, for all the good it will do—." The old man clapped his hands once. "You might as well give a name to the wet spot in the middle of the bed."

"But . . . But," objected one of the flannelled men at the end of the bar, "why do anything, then? You make it sound so . . . so hopeless."

The old man did not turn to look at this interlocutor. He ducked his head, rather, and lifted a single hand, while the other fell to his glass. "I didn't say anything about hopeless," he reminded everybody. "I just pointed out the obvious. There's no moral imperative, there's no blame, there's no . . ."

He didn't finish the sentence.

Everybody waited.

No more information seemed to be forthcoming.

The second man in a flannel shirt held two fingers aloft. "There's no tequila?"

"There is tequila," Bruce assured him.

"Top shelf," the man said.

Bruce went about his business.

A phone rang.

Yesterday, Klinger wouldn't have recognized it as the ring of a phone, let alone that the ringtone was "Creation of Tron," by Wendy Carlos.

Today? Different.

The ringtone sounded again, louder than the first time.

Lifting his drink to lips parched by loquacity, the old man paused.

Klinger looked around. The ringtone sounded a third time. He looked down. It was coming from his bag of clothing. The ringtone sounded a forth time. He bethought himself of the street door, not fifteen feet behind him. All he had to do was get up, leave the bag where it was, walk through the street door, and disappear into the heedless continuum.

"Answer that piece of shit for god's sakes," Bruce said, as he passed by on the other side of the bar bearing a tray with four brimming shot glasses, an ashtray full of lime wedges, and a salt shaker.

But it was raining. But he needed a drink. But, in the hotel just upstairs, not far away at all, barely far away enough to get any wetter than he already was, he was paid up for another week. But he needed to shut up this phone. He asked Bruce to bring him a Jameson, rocks, thinking to hell with appearances, it's not good to switch brands midstream, and he leaned to rummage in the bag. "Make it a double," he added, as his hand found the device. "Hello."

"Hi," she said.

"What is this phone doing in this bar?" he said.

"I . . . thought you could use a phone," she said. "Everybody needs a phone."

"I'm not everybody," Klinger told the phone, "and I don't need a phone."

Bruce came back, placed a coaster on the bar, set a glass half full of ice on the coaster, and dispensed a generous pour. Klinger stood on the lower rung of his stool and dug a twenty out of his damp britches. Bruce traded it for two of the dollar bills resulting from the transaction down the bar and turned to his register. Klinger pushed the two singles into the gutter on the opposite side of the bar and sat down again. Bruce dropped a ten next to Klinger's drink.

He didn't say another word. He sipped the drink. It was good. Not cold yet. Good. A shiver passed through him He'd intended to disappear into another part of the city, with his bag of laundry and his thousand dollars, but habit, rain, and, he was starting to realize, two days without sleep had brought him to here, to this place, to this moment.

He looked at the drink. He should have ordered a grog. Something hot. Something healthful. Something nurturing. A grog and some vitamin C, maybe.

He drained half the remaining drink and set it down.

"Doesn't your friend want his phone back?"

"He doesn't need it anymore," the voice said.

Klinger frowned.

"It's your phone, now." She hung up.

"Hello . . . ?" Klinger looked at the screen. Amid the myriad choices, selections and icons, a message informed him that the previous call had lasted one minute and thirty-two seconds.

Klinger put the phone on the bar and contemplated his drink.

Without warning the pain in his gut asserted itself. Just a twinge, really. A reminder.

Straight behind him the street door opened, admitted the hiss of passing tires on a wet street, and closed again.

The bar got quiet. The old man clasped two hands around his drink on the bar and stared at it. Bruce rang up his second sale and glanced over his shoulder. Both the two guys in flannel shirts, at the far end of the bar, glanced toward the front door, then conspicuously returned their attention to their tequilas.

Bruce, standing directly in front of Klinger, between him and the mirror behind the bottles behind the bar, occluded Klinger's view of the reflection of the street door.

No matter. The hand on Klinger's shoulder told him all he needed to know.

"Nice phone," said a voice. "High-end model."

Klinger didn't answer this.

"Yours?"

Klinger said nothing.

The fingers of the hand dug into the tender tissue,

exacerbated by tension and exhaustion, between Klinger's clavicle and his neck.

"No," Klinger evinced. "I found it. Out front. On the sidewalk."

A hand laid a second phone on the bar next to Phillip's phone. "See that app?" said a second voice.

"The fuck's a app?" Klinger heard himself saying.

"Going from the general to the particular," the second voice said, "it's a gizmo on that phone, there." A hand pointed to the second phone. "It tells ya where that phone, there," the hand pointed a finger at Phillip's phone, "is at."

"Oh," said Klinger sullenly. "Like WhereIz?"

"Hey," said the second voice. The back of a hand lightly flicked his shoulder. "That's the exact one."

That bitch, Klinger said to himself. That fucking bitch.

"A quick study," said the voice appurtenant to the hand on Klinger's shoulder.

"Turn around," said the second voice.

The hand on his shoulder helped him turn around. Klinger's wet ass squeaked on the barstool upholstery.

As cops go they read young. Both wore black baseball caps and vinyl anoraks, the one olive drab, the other blue. Unlike his partner, the younger of the two, the one with his hand on Klinger's shoulder affected no moustache. The trend must have faded, Klinger reflected. But these weren't your normal rode-hard, put-away-wet, worn-out and overworked bunko guys, either. Detectives, maybe. A cut above.

Down the bar, the two guys in flannel shirts finished their tequilas, set the empties on the plank, and made as if to leave.

Klinger squared off with the older cop. "Well?"

"It's about the phone," the guy said simply.

Klinger shook his head. "No, it's not about the phone."

The man shrugged. "Know a guy name of Phillip? Phillip Wong?"

Klinger shook his head.

"This used to be his phone."

"I found it." Klinger pointed. "On the sidewalk out front, about seven-thirty this morning." He almost added, And I told his girlfriend all about it. But he didn't add anything.

"This guy Wong?" the older cop said. "He got himself mugged."

"Sorry to hear about it."

"Just last night."

"Okay," Klinger said.

"In North Beach," the cop said.

Bruce moved down the bar, ostensibly to retrieve the four empty shot glasses.

"Been to North Beach lately?" the younger cop asked.

"People get mugged all the time." Klinger shrugged off the hand. "Especially in North Beach."

"That's true," the older cop conceded. "But usually, they don't get left for dead."

Klinger looked from the older cop to the other, then back. "Are you telling me I killed a guy for a cellphone?"

The cop touched both hands to his breast. "Did I say you killed him?"

"For what?" Klinger laughed without mirth. "For I should call my mother?"

"For you should call your bookie," the younger cop said. "Or maybe your lawyer."

"Hey," Klinger sneered, "it's not like it's a pair of sneakers."

Insofar as the younger cop failed to see the humor, he balled his fist and dropped his shoulder. Klinger took him seriously enough to wince, and then it was the younger cop's turn to sneer.

The older cop let the two face it off for a minute before he touched Klinger on the arm. "Take a look at this."

Klinger, who had allowed himself to glare at the younger cop, now glared at his partner. "At what?"

The older cop took up the second phone, swiped at its screen, then turned it so Klinger could see it.

Klinger glanced at it, looked at the younger cop, then at the older one.

"We can blow this up till it fits on the wall, if that's what you want," the older cop told him.

Klinger took a closer look. After a while he said, "Am I supposed to know what I'm looking at?"

The older cop said, "Let me zoom in a bit." He swiped at the screen. "How's that?"

Klinger saw a clipboard.

"It's a clipboard."

"Now we're talking," the cop said. He touched the screen. "And now?"

Klinger frowned. "It's the metal clip on a clipboard."

"Very good," the cop said. He turned the screen so that it faced him and touched it. "It's a spring clip. Made to grip stuff." He turned the screen around. "Can you see what's caught in it?"

As the screen turned, the image turned with it.

"It looks like a piece of tubing."

"Very good. And what about that piece of tubing?"

Klinger shook his head.

"It's bent double and crimped under the edge of the clipboard clip," the cop said.

Klinger stared.

"Very attentive," said the cop. "Now watch carefully."

Holding the cellphone so that everybody could see it, the cop drew his finger across the screen and, as he did so, the image tracked along the length of tubing, down to the lower edge of the bed, then up, foot by foot, over the satin trim at the edge of a blanket, until it terminated at the base of a ventilator mask. The fingers swiped and the image zoomed out until it was clear that ventilator was strapped to a man's face. The man's eyes were wide open, and they were sightless.

"Looks surprised, doesn't he," said the cop.

Klinger said nothing.

"The surprise that passeth all understanding," said the cop. He caused the image to zoom in, then zoom out. He held the phone too close to Klinger's face. "What do you think?"

"What do I think?" Klinger said, appalled. "I think the guy's dead."

"Brighter and brighter," said the younger cop.

"Know him?" asked the older cop. "The dead guy?"

No reaction was going to contravene what was coming, but Klinger shook his head anyway.

"He was the sole surviving witness to his own mugging," the older cop said. "Ring a bell?"

So that's why she was late.

"There was two muggers," the younger cop said. "One was a junkie pickpocket they called Frankie Geeze, on the street. Every hear of him?" He cast his eyes around the bar. "Anybody?"

No response. The two guys at the end of the bar said nothing. The old man tilted his glass on its coaster and said nothing. Bruce, who was polishing a glass, shrugged.

I've been had, Klinger blinked. Big time.

"Let me help." The cop with the telephone touched its screen a couple of times and presented the resulting jpeg to Klinger's inspection.

It was a very recent picture, but Klinger barely recognized Frankie.

Looking over Klinger's shoulder the younger cop stated the obvious. "Frankie don't look too good."

"I can do something about that." The older cop touched the phone and another image came up.

Frankie doesn't look too good in his mug shot either, Klinger thought, but at least he doesn't look dead.

"Know him?" asked the older cop.

Klinger shrugged. "I know a lot of guys."

"You." The cop showed the phone to Bruce. "Know him?"

Bruce pretended to study the image. He squinted, adjusted the distance of his face to the screen, changed the angle of incident light. Then he shook his head. "Nope."

"That's okay," the older cop said, not bothering to conceal his scorn. He touched the screen on his phone, it went dark, he put the phone away, he addressed Klinger: "When you found out he was alive, you had to take him out."

This took Klinger aback. "Who was alive?"

"The victim," the cop said. "He could identify you. You and your accomplice."

"Accomplice to what?"

"Why, to the mugging in North Beach," the cop said.

Klinger blinked. Then he nodded. "The mugging in North Beach . . ."

The younger cop smirked. "He's having trouble keeping his crimes straight."

"Don't worry," the older cop said, "you can't snitch out a dead guy, and a dead guy can't snitch out anybody." He held up Phillip's phone. "You can go to the death house with your head held high." He pretended to pause. "Dignity intact."

"Well?" The second cop leered.

"Won't you?" the older cop repeated.

Klinger could hardly hear them. She set me up and

dropped a dime on me, he was telling himself. She framed me.

"Don't even bother to deny it," the younger cop said. "An undercover guy saw you in here a couple of days ago with Frankie Geeze."

The older cop glared at his younger companion.

Klinger and Bruce exchanged a look. Bruce slid his eyes down the bar. The two guys in flannel shirts had found something interesting to discuss, and they had turned their backs to the rest of the room. Klinger frowned. Were the same two guys in here the other night? On the one hand they looked like a thousand other punks. On the other hand, they didn't look all that familiar. He frowned some more. Was that last night? This morning, even?

"That doesn't make any difference," the older cop told him. "We got you on a surveillance tape at the hospital. Too bad. I can't blame you for trying. It's hell to go down because one guy gets himself killed while he and his buddy are just trying to make a living." The cop made with a rictus smile, and his voice conveyed only contempt. "Simple hell."

"Yeah," the younger cop pseudo-sympathized, while bluffing past his gaff. "Pretty tough."

The older cop used his thumb and forefinger to pick up Phillip's cellphone by its diagonally opposite corners. The younger cop produced a padded envelope and opened its mouth, and the older cop dropped Phillip's cellphone into it. The younger cop sealed the envelope, produced a ballpoint pen and made a note on the flap, then slid the envelope into the side pocket of his anorak.

"Let's go," said the older cop.

They each took an arm and steered Klinger out the front door, where a black and white waited in the rain, steam lifting from its tailpipe.

Up the street idled another black and white, a third

idled beyond the crosswalk, an unmarked car with tinted windows blocked the bus stop across the intersection. There was an ambulance, too.

She's in the unmarked car, Klinger thought, as the two cops expertly fed him into the back seat of the black and white.

The old man had barely moved the whole time the cops were in the bar, not even to sip his drink.

"His laundry remains," he said to the row of bottles in front of the backbar mirror.

Bruce, who hadn't noticed, now walked down to the far end of the bar, rounded it, came back past the old man, and retrieved the large, wet shopping bag that contained Klinger's recently purchased clothes.

The two guys at the dogleg in the bar watched and said nothing.

Holding it away from his legs so they wouldn't get wet, Bruce walked the bag to a closet next to the toilets. As he opened the door the bottom fell out of the bag. Shit, said Bruce softly. He lifted the pile of wet clothes with the toe of his boot, into a corner of the closet next to a mop bucket. He dropped the bottomless bag on top of them, retrieved a filthy mop from the bucket, and closed the door.

"His laundry remains to remind us of who he was," the old man muttered thoughtfully to his drink. He took a sip. "I might have to revise my theory."

Bruce mopped up the water on the floor and swabbed the wet stool with the rag that hung from his waistband.

When Bruce had replaced the mop in the closet and resumed his station behind the bar, the old man rattled the ice in the glass and pushed the empty across the plank.

"Hit me again."

A Conversation with Jim Nisbet, Patrick Marks, and Gent Sturgeon

Patrick: What book are we here to discuss?

Jim: *Sneetch World.*

Patrick: So we are sitting here at an undisclosed location in Hayes Valley, San Francisco, with Jim Nisbet, Patrick Marks, copublisher and proprietor of The Green Arcade, and Gent Sturgeon, who did the cover art.

Jim: Fabulous cover. I love that cover. And I am a man of many covers—like Frank Sinatra.

Patrick: Well, as you know, I have been a lounge singer and occasionally I will have someone come up and say, accusingly: "You only do covers." So what's so bad about Cole Porter and Burt Bacharach?

Jim: But you have to give it up to Frank, he would always call out the author and composer of the tune. He would always give credit.

Patrick: *Snitch World*—the title?

Jim: I had an old friend who was a professional thief. He is now deceased. And he died on the outside. In fact, he never did time. He would see something outrageous on TV and he would shake his head, and say, "It's a snitch world, man, that is all there is to it."

Patrick: The main character of the book, Klinger, also never did time—

Jim: That's true. All the people around him have.

Patrick: The world of *Snitch World* seems to be a world of losers surrounded by gross criminality. The people who are seemingly successful, like the techies, are living a doubtful existence. It sort of mimics our world here in San Francisco, where we are surrounded by money and technology and you wonder who the real losers are.

Jim: The losers are the people who used to live here. The blue-collar world that used to be San Francisco when I came here, in 1966. The longshoremen. Harry Bridges was still alive. There were railyards and a working waterfront.

Patrick: You mention Harry Bridges in the book, do you remember?

Jim: Yeah, I do. That guy Jimmy that Klinger meets on a bench in Washington Square Park—that is a true anecdote. I met this guy. He had on a blue blazer. His wife came tottering along with him and she sat him down on a bench on the northeast corner of the park, facing the sun and Coit Liquor. It's pretty much like it went down. I tweaked it a little. I had the guy buy Klinger lunch and tell his story. The lunch is made up, but the story isn't. He was a very interesting guy, like you used to meet all the time in this town. He said he came to San Francisco in a boxcar and the first person he met was Harry Bridges, who put him on the docks, and the next thing he knew he was getting his head busted, and having all this fun. He met his wife. He just said it was the most amazing place he had ever been. He never left. And after the war, the babies started coming, and he got into advertising and did well. He was retired and he ate lunch every Saturday afternoon at Moose's. It was just a classic San Francisco character-slash-experience that I never run into anymore. I'm that guy now.

Patrick: Oh boy.

Jim: Except for the advertising and the money.

Patrick: What's the name of the bar they hang out in, in *Snitch World*?

Jim: The Hawse Hole. Remember when that girl asks,

"What's a hawse hole, anyway?" And he doesn't answer the question. You looked it up right?

Patrick: I didn't. But I was going to!

Jim: Hah!

Patrick: Bad publisher.

Jim: Well, it's the hole on the bow of a ship through which runs the anchor cable or chain. There used to be a joint on Larkin . . .

Patrick: The Gangway.

Jim: Yes. The bow of the ship sticking out onto the street.

Patrick: Remember that place on Powell Street with the whole damned boat from the nineteenth century—Bernstein's?

Jim: No, but Ferlinghetti tells the story, when he got off the boat, when he got back from France with all that Jacques Prévert in his seabag, and walked up Market Street and he said San Francisco was the goddamndest place he'd ever seen.

Gent: He had the same experience a lot of GIs had.

Patrick: My dad was the same way.

Jim: All those bars on Market Street that went all the way through to Stevenson Street. And you got a shot with a half pint of beer for eighty cents.

Patrick: Did you ever go to Day's Bar? It was the biggest bar in the West. Supposedly someone bought the bar itself and sent it off to Nevada when they razed the building. Hey, let's get back to the damned book.

Jim: This is authentication. This is not a nostalgia trip, it's a reality check. It's kinda like Rebecca Solnit did that in that book when she went around to all those San Francisco locations, like the 6 Gallery, which was up on Fillmore, which is now a rug store. It's not nostalgia, it's checking what's gone. In many ways, San Francisco was a hard town in those days.

Patrick: We liked that.

Jim: And you could be yourself here. A lot of stuff happened to me in those years that doesn't seem to happen anymore. But like the night I ran out of gas out on Sloat and a drunk gave me the keys to his car. And said to be back in an hour or he would call the cops, if I didn't come back to the bar. I had to go to hell and back to get gas, and put it in my truck on the Great Highway.

Patrick: So is that Snitch World?

Jim: Well, no, I think it evolved from that into the world *Snitch World*'s Georgie saw, where people would dime each other, drop a dime on their mother if there's twenty cents in it. I don't want to lay too heavy a metaphysical trip on the book, but it does seem to ring a few chimes like that. Things are more competitive. That solidarity that the Wobblies had going, where it would all go down. In those days, the newspaper—the *newspapers*, there were five or six of them—the cops, the establishment, all together were down on the guys that worked on the docks. They were completely willing to shoot them, bust their heads, put 'em in jail, and do whatever it took to keep them from organizing, to keep them from stopping work, from striking for better conditions, better wages. The entire establishment was against them. Then there was a time when it was a little more accepted, although Harry Bridges, because he was a commie, was always on the outside. And the vestiges of that are still around. I never knew Harry Bridges. He was around when I came here, it's true. And he lived a good long time to put the finger in the eye of the establishment. Which is always there to have a finger in its eye.

I knew a guy named Jim Hamilton, who died around three years ago, who was a longshoreman and who cowrote *Cross of Iron* with Sam Peckinpah and who turned me onto that terrific novel, by the way [*The Willing Flesh* by Willi Heinrich]. He did a documentary on Bridges, which I've never seen but which is apparently quite good. Jim was so modest and so past all that stuff. I said, "Hey Jim, you know, I watched *Cross of Iron* again a while back and noticed it was based on a novel." And he said, "Oh yeah, that's a tough book." That's all he said. Except later he said, "That book is all about class."

Patrick: We just watched Renoir's *Grand Illusion* again. Talk about class.

Gent: I just read *The Red and the Black*. Class.

Jim: Oh god, Stendhal is fantastic. We could spend a whole night talking about Stendhal.

Patrick: But we can't get too far from *Snitch World*.

Jim: I have the Norton Critical Edition of *The Red and the Black*. Their one of Chekov short stories is fantastic. It's a selection, but it's chronological and it's just an unbelievable crescendo of achievement. Does Norton still exist?

Patrick: Very much so.

Jim: Good good good.

Patrick: Maybe your next book could be from Norton.

Jim: Let's finish this one first.

Patrick: So you want to talk about publishing for a little bit?

Jim: Well, *Old and Cold* and *Spider's Cage* just came in the mail. They changed the title of *Ulysses' Dog* to *Spider's Cage*. And they jacked the price: $15.95 for a slim-pickins paperback.

Gent: Did I ever tell you I read Sandro's book? [Sandro Veronesi's *Quiet Chaos*]

Jim: Yes, you did, and I remember how much you liked it. Did you ever give it to Lawrence [Ferlinghetti]? That was the idea. That's a really good book.

Gent: Yes, I gave to him but I never heard about it. That was really a good book. I was amazed by it, actually.

Jim: When I first met Sandro, he had never written a book.

Gent: He pulled something off that was quite extraordinary. We've sold a lot of them at City Lights.

Jim: Oh, great—I'll tell him.

Patrick: It's published by Ecco. Hey, *Snitch World*, ahem, is published by PM Press and The Green Arcade. What do you think of that?

Jim: I think it's great. I love having a martini with my publisher and my editor and my cover artist, who are my friends, and it just gets friendlier. And there's no bullshit involved and there's no New York involved.

Patrick: But what about the dough, though?

Jim: The dough is small. [All laugh. Dexter Brown, Jr., the dog, barks.] But, as my friend Alastair Johnston used to say, "The hand is always bigger than the money."

Patrick: I wanted to ask you about literary versus genre writing, you being known as a noirist. Don't you think that writing is just writing?

Jim: Oh yeah. But all genre guys say that. But hardly any writing is Richard Ford.

All: U-uuuuu.

Jim: You know, I ain't got him from square one. I don't get that guy. Except as a sleep aid.

Patrick: You know I am expanding the Arcade a bit to have more fiction—hopefully not soporifics—and more noir.

Jim: You have a lot of noir titles—you have a lot of great books in there.

Patrick: In the old days of San Francisco, or maybe the medium-old days of San Francisco, the neighborhood around the store was called the hub. And actually, The Green Arcade was the Hub Tavern.

Jim: No!

Patrick: Yeah, baby.

Jim: No wonder the vibes are so good in there.

Patrick: So maybe the back of the store could be your Noir Hub.

Jim: You have that urban theme thing going on—

Patrick: The Noir Hub is the shadow cast by the Urban Studies section.

Jim: You should be in marketing.

Patrick: But like I was saying, it is kind of a contradiction saying "writing is writing" and then fencing off this area where the Jim Nisbet books go.

Jim: Hey, fences were made for jumping. But you should look at the Black Lizard list.

Patrick: You were a Black Lizard. I really miss the original Black Lizard. Tell me about it, the ye olde days.

Jim: Barry Gifford curated this collection, brought back a lot of noir superstars, for lack of better term, beginning in the early eighties and it ran until 1990, when it sold out to Random House.

Patrick: Jim Thompson was the biggie?

Jim: When Jim Thompson died in the early '70s, he was totally out of print, except for maybe *The Killer Inside Me* and *Pop. 1280*. As was David Goodis, as was Peter Rabe, as was Dan Marlowe—*The Name of the Game Is Death*. A great novel, just great. And there are a lot of them. *Violent Saturday*, you remember W.L. Heath? These cons show up in this little hick town and try to be inconspicuous for a week while they case the bank. And then they blow the job and kill a pregnant schoolteacher—

Patrick: I *hate* when that happens. Hey, speaking of school, did you hear they paroled one of the Chowchilla kidnappers?

Jim: Oh my god, I didn't think those guys would ever get out.

Patrick: I think they should have let him out.

Jim: Was he the kid?

Patrick: He was the younger brother. The mastermind will most likely never get out. Like my friend Sin Soracco [author of *Low Bite*] once said, "About five percent of those in prison ought to be in prison."

Jim: Still, that was an outrage, burying that school bus. And wasn't it the teacher who escaped through the top of the bus?

Patrick: No, it was the driver.

Gent: I'm surprised they never made a movie out if it.

Patrick: They did, with Karl Malden. But there was a book. Not Richard Ford, who's the other one?

Jim: Tom McGuane. [All laugh]

Patrick: No, the other other one.

Jim: "McGuane's the name; writin's the game." Yeah, that and real estate.

Patrick: Hey did you hear McMurtry just had this big sale out thar in Texas at his book town?

Jim: Is he done? He said he was done.

Gent: I think he was just reducing his stock.

Patrick: I wish I could have gone.

Jim: His store in DC was fabulous. I sat and talked with him. It was very interesting. There was a larger store with a little living room, a couple couches and tables. And then across the street, the door was open, was a little building that had all the art books in it, and the door was open and no one attended it. And he would sit in the living room, surrounded by books, and sort of keep an eye—very casual. And I went in there and said hello to him. Was I published yet? I don't remember. This woman from England came in and had this list of American novels that some friend of her had recommended that she pick up when she was in America. And it was an amazing list. And Larry McMurtry knew every book on it. Like that guy Steele. He taught creative writing at the University of North Carolina, Max Steele. I never read any of his books, but Larry knew them. McMurtry knew who the guy was and had read the books.

Gent: And he had all the books in the store?

Jim: He didn't have them all. Actually, we got completely sidetracked talking about poetry—Gary Snyder was on the list. He had *Rip Rap* and *Cold Mountain Poems* in stock—nice clean, used copies. For a tasty price—not too bad. Point is he had 'em.

Patrick: So what were we talking about?

Jim: The noir section in the store. So you look at the Black Lizard list and see what's still in print and you look for the others used and you get this tasty little section going. Curated strictly by quality.

Patrick: Kayo Books is great—

Jim: Just great. I went there with Dennis McMillan, the publisher. Dennis found very obscure stuff. Some of the books that are collectible are cheap, like Charles Williams, because no one knows what they are. And there are several black writers that did these tough books.

Patrick: Gary Phillips is an expert on that.

Jim: And Dennis McMillan knows all about it.

Patrick: You seem to know all about the down-and-out world. In *Snitch World*, the main character Klinger gets screwed over—

Jim: And snitched out. He is very busy screwing himself over.

Patrick: I like all the San Francisco stuff.

Jim: We have all been wandering around North Beach drunk in the middle of the night and found these strange places. That local stuff is wonderful because there's a very interesting thing that happens when you ask, "What is this place really like? I don't remember how I wound up on this corner." Well, you got dipped on Broadway, and then they went down to the corner to divide the money. And in *Snitch World* it turned out, or course, that Frankie had lifted the guy's phone Which is the real issue. He didn't give a shit about the money.

Patrick: Which is this whole world of phones and apps.

Jim: About which Klinger knows nothing.

Patrick: There seems to be a digital divide.

Jim: Not really. Anybody can jump in and anybody can be left out. There are plenty of people who want to be left out. You know, we were talking about print versus tablet media. I have a cabinet shop, for many years, and one of the great things about having a cabinet shop is print catalogs that mean something, that have stuff in them that you actually need and want and buy. And some, like the Granger catalog is something like two thousand pages. It's a brick.

Patrick: I'm surprised they still make those.

Jim: They stopped. Here's the point. A couple of years went by after they stopped, I get this CD-ROM in the mail. And the assumption is you have a computer that will run the CD-ROM. And then if you wanted to browse the catalog, you're clicking on the arrow and it's not like sitting on the head with the Granger catalog, just flipping through it. So then they got rid of the CD-ROM and now they had e-catalogs. It's all not-do-ably slow. It's just a drag, no matter how you tart it up. So now, after ten years or so, all of a sudden, they are starting to come back with the catalogs.

Patrick: From e-books to print!

Jim: I think there's a big possibility that the wave has crested and that it is going to recede. And what's going to be left is independent bookstores and independent presses that know what they are doing. And the big publishers who have hedged their bets while dealing with Mister Bezos. Don't forget, there was a time when Borders was the elephant of capitalism that was tromping on everybody. And why shouldn't it happen to Amazon?

Patrick: Too big to fail.

Jim: Too big to not fail. So anyway, what does *Snitch World* have to do with this?

Patrick: Well, you often concern your characters and plot with technology, and there are some technological similarities between the two books we did together: *A Moment of Doubt* and *Snitch World*, although *A Moment of Doubt* was written in the '80s and this book is from a year or so ago.

Jim: *A Moment of Doubt* was written in 1982, so thirty years ago. I don't know where the subject matter comes from. And it's hard not to read the technology as somewhat adversarial. Like there's such a thing as being up against Stalin, although you'll never meet him, and his machine will just crush you, or do whatever it wants to you. You'll have that 1984 experience or even the Kafkaesque experience, where you don't understand why it's happening; you just understand that it is happening. You don't know who is doing it or why. And technology is a similar thing. In its way, it is a force of history. Tolstoy made this argument, that humans are just helpless in the face of history. That long, insufferable last hundred pages of *War and Peace*. He calls it God, but the previous eleven hundred pages were about Napoleon. It's like, hey, man, make up your mind! Is it Steve Jobs, or is it technology? And you know Bezos is not in my game. Although he's fucking with me more than Steve ever did. Steve made my life interesting. I still have three Windows98 PCs that I do CAD and my accounting on. And if can, I have a DOS machine that I do my writing on. And I got reasons for all that stuff. But here's an iBook right here.

Patrick: You are a techy nerd. Let's face it.

Jim: I know about this stuff to a certain degree, it's true. I've got way better reasons to be acting this way than they're giving me to act some other way. Except the fact that I'm superannuated, which I am becoming anyway.

Patrick: The technological aspect in your books is a dialectic.

Jim: It's the Other. I don't approach it that way.

Patrick: But there's a process—

Jim: That implies that they are talking to each another.

Patrick: That happens, I hear I hear.

Jim: Klinger's not talking to it.

Patrick: But he is determined by it.

Jim: In spite of the fact that he doesn't even know what's happening.

Gent: Is it appropriate to see the historical lines, like you were talking earlier? Klinger belongs to a world that has ceased to be, but he is still alive.

Patrick: We are all part of some lost world, San Francisco or otherwise.

Gent: Like you were talking earlier—

Jim: Like Harry Bridges—San Francisco used to be a blue-collar town. Try to find a blue collar now.

Gent: It disappears, but you are still here. I know so many people like that.

Jim: Gent, I can so totally go down with that. Even a blue-collar criminal can't make it in this town.

Patrick: But you point out that a white-collar criminal is insanely successful.

Jim: And sophisticated. Although the wire guy, the dipper, did okay. I'm speaking from experience. I've been dipped, on Broadway. I was carousing on Broadway with Andrei Codrescu, Barry Gifford, and Davia Nelson and was going from Tosca to that joint that was across from Enrico's for a while.

Gent: Swiss Louie's.

Jim: Nah nah nah, way after that; no one remembers Swiss Louie's.

Patrick: The Black Cat.

Jim: Chat Noir. It lasted a couple years. They were all up there and had a bunch of booze and stuff and I lingered at Tosca over my martini. I still had a full martini and I was loaded and didn't care about eating. I finished it off and wandered up Broadway and there were various things that happened, but at some point a very nicely dressed little man came up behind me and brushed by me and said, "Oh, can you tell me how to get to the Ferry Building?" Just like in the book, except there weren't two of them. I remember the moon rising up over the end of Broadway. I told him how to get there, and he said he had an appointment and he left. I had decided not to eat with my people and I had walked almost back to Columbus toward my truck when the light went on. I wasn't that fuckin' loaded. I had on a suit jacket and a sweater and jeans with a horizontal pocket. I went in my pocket and the two hundred bucks less some drinks was gone. Folded just like I always do. I couldn't believe it. It was good. It was like magic. About a week or so later I was with my friend George Malone, Shanty Malone in the Herb Caen column. He used to own the River Inn in Big Sur. Longtime hustler, con man. A dear friend of mine. And I explained this to him and I asked him what had happened.

Gent: How'd he get his hand in your pocket?

Jim: "Jimmy," he said, "he's a dipper." I said, "What the fuck is that?" He said that sometimes they call him a wireman. He's got a piece of wire that's got an "L" on the bottom of it. "And he checked you out, man. He marked you. He saw you buy a drink a couple times and you always went into the same pocket. Man, you didn't have a chance. And you were loaded." And I said, "Wow, man, that's pretty good." And he said, "Yeah, they're all very good. But the problem with those guys is that they're all fucking hop-heads; you can't trust 'em."

Patrick: What are you going to trust 'em for?

Jim: Well, you know, guys partner up and stuff and they never snitch. They're all junkies and they make good money doing this. They only gotta dip one or two guys like me and they're good for a couple days. 'Cause they got a habit. It's like, I ran into an old friend of mine and I said, "Hey what are you up to?" And he said, "About sixty a day."

Patrick: You put that in *Snitch World*. Except it was a hundred. Pretty funny. There is a lot of hilarious stuff in the book. Like the scene of the nightmare where he's digging under the cemetery with the Chinese guy in Colorado.

Jim: That's another true story.

Patrick: What? Wait a minute!

Jim: It was told to me on a ski lift in Colorado. A place called Ski Cooper. All these stories, I left out a lot. Because of my narrative I was servicing. But in those days I had a small pickup truck and I was winter camping and skiing all over Colorado and New Mexico. March and April. I had my dog, pH. We slept in the back of my truck. Not even a camper shell. Brown rice and tea. Living outside. I would find a ski hill with nobody on it and I would just go skiing for half a day. I wound up in Leadville and I found this place called Ski Cooper. It's in this big long flat valley, and it turned out that the United States Army trained their ski troops there during World War II. And when it was over they leveled all the buildings, which explained this big unblemished valley that was completely filled with snow when I was there. And they had this very modest ski hill that had a rope tow still. And I found a place called the Little Tundra Motel. I stayed for a week and they finally bumped me out because an evangelist choir had booked the whole place six months in advance. I was reading Tanizaki, *The Makioka Sisters*, the whole time. So I'm on a chair and here's a guy, breathing hard, because he only has one lung, see. Leadville is the highest town in the United States. And it's played out. There's a closed-down molybdenum mine north of the town, and the pickup truck of whoever owns it is parked in front of all this gear and they're waiting for the molybdenum deposit in Congo, or wherever the fuck it is, to play out, so they can reopen it. Leadville was silver and gold at one time.

Patrick: That was Horace Taber and Baby Doe—

Jim: I wanna hear that story. So this guy was winded, on the chairlift, and we started talking and his story is he was from Leadville. A Vietnam vet, and he got shot up in Vietnam, that's where the lung went, and got airlifted back here to Alameda, and was in a busload of wounded vets on the way from Alameda to Letterman Hospital in San Francisco—which is now George Lucas's Letterman Digital Arts Center—and during Vietnam it also had a psych ward. On the Bay Bridge demonstrators turned the bus over and he and this one other vet who still had their arms and legs got out and pounded the shit out of every demonstrator they could get their hands on. Until the cops broke it up. Okay, so that was one ski lift story. We ski down the hill together. So on the next trip up he asks me what I do, and I mumble I'm a writer. And he gives me his card and it turns out he is a dynamiter. He makes his living, such as it is, dynamiting. He learned demolition in the service and once in a while he sets charges. For roads or mines. He was in AA and had a twenty-four-hour tureen of coffee going in this big Victorian in the middle of Leadville. And anyone who came through could get a cup of coffee from him, drunk or sober, vet or not. And he had huskies on the roof, three stories up, looking down on Leadville. At that time Leadville was pretty moribund.

Gent: It don't look too good now.

Jim: So, he had become a drunk, he had become homeless, he had gotten cleaned up, and he came back to Leadville, adjusting to the altitude in stages, because of the one lung, beginning here, at sea level. So we're going back up on the lift again. I said, "So, do you really make a living blowing up shit for mines and roads, and stuff?" he said, "Well, to tell you the truth, I got a buddy, and he's a vet, too." You know, Leadville, like a lot of places in California and the West, is honeycombed with tunnels that Chinese laborers would dig on their days off. They would just follow seams looking for gold. He said, "My buddy and I, we got a pretty good map of what goes on under Leadville." It's all owned and forbidden. But they had a place on the outside of town, this cut-bank, with all these bushes on it, where you could go into the tunnel system. And it's dicey, because the tunnels weren't at all reinforced. And he said they would get out enough nuggets every year to supplement the dynamiting income.

Patrick: There are hundreds if not thousands of people living in the boony wildernesses of the Sierra.

Jim: So, he told me that the first time he took his buddy, with picks and headlamps and the map, they got into this one place. There were boards on the roof of the tunnel, which was rare, because the Chinese had not reinforced the tunnels, and the wood was fairly rotten and they chipped away at it and it caved in and it was all bones. They were under the Leadville cemetery. It was a long time before that story worked its way into the greater narrative of *Snitch World*.

Patrick: Well, hell, I'm glad it did.

About the Author

San Francisco writer Jim Nisbet has published thirteen novels, including the acclaimed *Lethal Injection*. He has also published five volumes of poetry and a nonfiction title. *Dark Companion* was shortlisted for the 2006 Hammett Prize for Literary Excellence in A Mystery Novel, and *Windward Passage* won the Science Fiction Award of the 2010 San Francisco Book Festival. Ten of his novels have been published in French, six in Italian, and these are constellated by a miscellany of translations into German, Japanese, Polish, Hungarian, Greek, Russian, and Romanian. One of his current projects is the complete translation of Charles Baudelaire's 1861 edition of *Les Fleurs du mal*. Another is a new novel, currently titled *You Don't Pencil*, which he is considering changing to *Stuck on Stupid*. Learn more at www.noirconeville.com.

Credo of The Green Arcade
The Green Arcade, a curated bookstore, specializes in sustainability, from the built environment to the natural world. The Green Arcade is a meeting place for rebels, flaneurs, farmers, and architects: those who build, inhabit, and add something valuable to the world.

The Green Arcade
1680 Market Street
San Francisco, CA 94102-5949
www.thegreenarcade.com

ABOUT PM PRESS

PM Press was founded at the end of 2007 by a small collection of folks with decades of publishing, media, and organizing experience. PM Press co-conspirators have published and distributed hundreds of books, pamphlets, CDs, and DVDs. Members of PM have founded enduring book fairs, spearheaded victorious tenant organizing campaigns, and worked closely with bookstores, academic conferences, and even rock bands to deliver political and challenging ideas to all walks of life. We're old enough to know what we're doing and young enough to know what's at stake.

We seek to create radical and stimulating fiction and non-fiction books, pamphlets, T-shirts, visual and audio materials to entertain, educate and inspire you. We aim to distribute these through every available channel with every available technology — whether that means you are seeing anarchist classics at our bookfair stalls; reading our latest vegan cookbook at the café; downloading geeky fiction e-books; or digging new music and timely videos from our website.

PM Press is always on the lookout for talented and skilled volunteers, artists, activists and writers to work with. If you have a great idea for a project or can contribute in some way, please get in touch.

PM Press
PO Box 23912
Oakland, CA 94623
www.pmpress.org

FRIENDS OF PM PRESS

These are indisputably momentous times—the financial system is melting down globally and the Empire is stumbling. Now more than ever there is a vital need for radical ideas.

In the six years since its founding—and on a mere shoestring—PM Press has risen to the formidable challenge of publishing and distributing knowledge and entertainment for the struggles ahead. With over 250 releases to date, we have published an impressive and stimulating array of literature, art, music, politics, and culture. Using every available medium, we've succeeded in connecting those hungry for ideas and information to those putting them into practice.

Friends of PM allows you to directly help impact, amplify, and revitalize the discourse and actions of radical writers, filmmakers, and artists. It provides us with a stable foundation from which we can build upon our early successes and provides a much-needed subsidy for the materials that can't necessarily pay their own way. You can help make that happen—and receive every new title automatically delivered to your door once a month—by joining as a Friend of PM Press. And, we'll throw in a free T-shirt when you sign up.

Here are your options:

- **$25 a month** Get all books and pamphlets plus 50% discount on all webstore purchases

- **$40 a month** Get all PM Press releases (including CDs and DVDs) plus 50% discount on all webstore purchases

- **$100 a month** Superstar—Everything plus PM merchandise, free downloads, and 50% discount on all webstore purchases

For those who can't afford $25 or more a month, we're introducing **Sustainer Rates** at $15, $10 and $5. Sustainers get a free PM Press T-shirt and a 50% discount on all purchases from our website.

Your Visa or Mastercard will be billed once a month, until you tell us to stop. Or until our efforts succeed in bringing the revolution around. Or the financial meltdown of Capital makes plastic redundant. Whichever comes first.

with PM Press
A Moment of Doubt
Jim Nisbet

ISBN: 978-1-60486-307-9
$13.95   144 pages

A Moment of Doubt is at turns hilarious, thrilling and obscene. Jim Nisbet's novella is ripped from the zeitgeist of the 80s, and set in a sex-drenched San Francisco, where the computer becomes the protagonist's co-conspirator and both writer and machine seem to threaten the written word itself. The City as whore provides a backdrop oozing with drugs, poets and danger. Nisbet has written a mad-cap meditation on the angst of a writer caught in a world where the rent is due, new technology offers up illicit ways to produce the latest bestseller, and the detective and other characters of the imagination might just sidle up to the bar and buy you a drink in real life. The world of *A Moment of Doubt* is the world of phone sex, bars and bordellos, AIDS and the lure of hacking. Coming up against the rules of the game—the detective genre itself, has never been such a nasty and gender defying challenge.

Plus: An interview with Jim Nisbet, who is "Still too little read in the United States, it's a joy for us that Nisbet has been recognized here . . ."
Regards: Le Mouvement des Idées

"*He is as weird as the world. And for some readers, that's a quality to cherish. It's as if Nisbet inhabited and wrote from a world right next to ours, only weirder.*"
— Rick Kleffel, bookotron.com

"*Missing any book by Nisbet should be considered a crime in all 50 states and maybe against humanity.*"
— Bill Ott, *Booklist*

"*With Nisbet, you know you can expect anything and you're never disappointed.*"
— *Le Figaro*

"*Jim Nisbet is a poet . . . [who] resembles no other crime fiction writer. He mixes the irony of Dantesque situations with lyric narration, and achieves a luxuriant cocktail that truly leaves the reader breathless.*"
— *Drood's Review of Mysteries*

with PM Press
Edge City
Sin Soracco

ISBN: 978-1-60486-503-5
$16.95   200 pages

Edge City, from the author of *Low Bite*, takes place in an every-noir-city (a thinly veiled portrait of San Francisco's North Beach) and its newest resident is Reno, an angry fledgling just hatched out of prison. Getting out is like a weird dream, and the streets of the City are a muddle of sensations pooling around her.

First there's the bustle—everybody busy with mysterious businesses—an amplifying racket of choices. Staggering out onto the late night streets of the City, Reno ends up at the infamous Istanbul Club: dim lights, Arabic music and the sensual Su'ad dancing. Music, booze, babes and drugs: what more could a felonious girl want?

She encounters Huntington, the poisonous charmer who lives above the Club—perverse and powerful in the way only the wealthy can be. Eddie, the underage bartender, is happy to chemically enhance every waking moment. Slowmotion, the sound light technician, huge and darkly mysterious, has connections to people and places that Reno didn't even know existed. Slowmotion's elegant friend, Poppy, offers mental transport to realms beyond Xanadu; in her little valise there's everything necessary for any trip, including the hallucinogenic "Teeth of Idi Amin."

The owner of the club, handsome gambler Sinclair, hires Reno to waitress. Grumbling, drinking, snarling and swearing, Reno bangs her way through everyone else's complicated plans, entangling herself in a byzantine labyrinth of betrayal, revenge, general mayhem, and yes, good times.

"Brilliant… Edge City is truly an extraordinary book in every way: story, people, atmosphere, writing."
— Hubert Selby, Jr., author of *Last Exit to Brooklyn*

"Sin Soracco cooks! Her writing is beyond hip—it struts and whistles down the last dark mile. Edge City, like her Low Bite, is the bad girl's version of Mean Streets, an unbeatable double-feature for the fearless."
— Barry Gifford, author of *Wild at Heart*

"Dark and sultry… an illuminating view of hell as a nightclub that never closes."
— New York Times

with PM Press
Low Bite
Sin Soracco

ISBN: 978-1-60486-226-3
$14.95   144 pages

Low Bite: Sin Soracco's prison novel about
survival, dignity, friendship, and insubordination.
The view from inside a women's prison isn't a
pretty one, and Morgan, the narrator, knows that
as well as anyone. White, female, 26, convicted
of nighttime breaking and entering with force, she works in the prison
law library, giving legal counsel of more-or-mostly-less usefulness to
other convicts. More useful is the hootch stash she keeps behind the law
books.

And she has plenty of enemies—like Johnson, the lesbian-hating warden,
and Alex, the "pretty little dude" lawyer who doesn't like her free legal
advice. Then there's Rosalie and Birdeye—serious rustlers whose loyalty
lasts about as long as their cigarettes hold out. And then there's China:
Latina, female, 22, holding US citizenship through marriage, convicted
of conspiracy to commit murder—a dangerous woman who is safer
in prison than she is on the streets. They're all trying to get through
without getting caught or going straight, but there's just one catch—a
bloodstained bank account that everybody wants, including some players
on the outside. *Low Bite*: an underground classic reprinted at last and the
first title in the new imprint from The Green Arcade.

"*Vicious, funny, cunning, ruthless, explicit… a tough original look at inside
loves and larcenies.*"
— Kirkus Reviews

"*Where else can you find the grittiness of girls-behind-bars mixed with
intelligence, brilliant prose, and emotional ferocity? Sin Soracco sets the
standard for prison writing. Hardboiled and with brains!*"
— Peter Maravelis, editor *San Francisco Noir* 1 and 2

"*Tells a gripping story concerning a group of women in a California prison:
their crimes, their relationships, their hopes and dreams.*"
— Publishers Weekly

"*Sin Soracco is the original Black Lizard. Low Bite will take a chunk out of
your leg if not your heart. Read it, it will devour you.*"
— Barry Gifford, author *Port Tropique*, Founder Black Lizard Books

with PM Press
Against Architecture

the green arcade

Franco La Cecla

Translated by Mairin O'Mahony

ISBN: 978-1-60486-406-9
$14.95   144 pages

First published in 2008, (as *Contro l'architettura*),
Against Architecture has been translated into
French and Greek, with editions forthcoming in
Polish and Portuguese. The book is a passionate
and erudite charge against the celebrities of the current architectural
world, the "archistars." According to Franco La Cecla, architecture has
lost its way and its true function, as the archistars use the cityscape to
build their brand, putting their stamp on the built environment with no
regard for the public good.

More than a diatribe against the trade for which he trained, Franco La
Cecla issues a call to rethink urban space, to take our cities back from
what he calls Casino Capitalism, which has left a string of failed urban
projects, from the Sagrera of Barcelona to the expansion of Columbia
University in New York City. As he comments throughout on the works
of past and present masters of urban and landscape writing, including
Robert Byron, Mike Davis, and Rebecca Solnit, Franco La Cecla has given
us a book that will take an important place in our public discourse.

*"To tell the truth, Franco La Cecla is not wrong. There is too much building,
sometimes only to put a signature, a stamp on a spot, without any worry
about the people who are going to live there. In other situations it is easy to
be used by the institutions that support speculation. It is the reason why I
refused many projects, because, I am lucky—and I can choose."*
— Renzo Piano in *La Repubblica*

*"La Cecla's book is a delight, in the way that he dismantles the glory of the
'archistar' in their proud myopic grandeur that totally ignores people and
their rights to a better urban life."*
— Sebastian Courtois, *La Reforme*

The Jook

Gary Phillips

ISBN: 978-1-60486-040-5
$15.95   256 pages

Zelmont Raines has slid a long way since
his ability to jook, to out maneuver his
opponents on the field, made him a Super Bowl
winning wide receiver, earning him lucrative
endorsement deals and more than his share
of female attention. But Zee hasn't always been good at saying no,
so a series of missteps involving drugs, a paternity suit or two, legal
entanglements, shaky investments and recurring injuries have virtually
sidelined his career.

That is until Los Angeles gets a new pro franchise, the Barons, and
Zelmont has one last chance at the big time he dearly misses. Just as it
seems he might be getting back in the flow, he's enraptured by Wilma
Wells, the leggy and brainy lawyer for the team—who has a ruthless
game plan all her own. And it's Zelmont who might get jooked.

*"Phillips, author of the acclaimed Ivan Monk series, takes elements of Jim
Thompson (the ending), black-exploitation flicks (the profanity-fueled
dialogue), and* Penthouse *magazine (the sex is anatomically correct) to
create an over-the-top violent caper in which there is no honor, no respect,
no love, and plenty of money. Anyone who liked George Pelecanos' King
Suckerman is going to love this even-grittier take on many of the same
themes."*
— Wes Lukowsky, *Booklist*

*"Enough gritty gossip, blistering action and trash talk to make real life L.A.
seem comparatively wholesome."*
— Kirkus Reviews

*"Gary Phillips writes tough and gritty parables about life and death on the
mean streets—a place where sometimes just surviving is a noble enough
cause. His is a voice that should be heard and celebrated. It rings true once
again in* The Jook, *a story where all of Phillips' talents are on display."*
— Michael Connelly, author of the Harry Bosch books

I-5

Summer Brenner

ISBN: 978-1-60486-019-1
$15.95   256 pages

A novel of crime, transport, and sex, *I-5* tells the bleak and brutal story of Anya and her journey north from Los Angeles to Oakland on the interstate that bisects the Central Valley of California.

Anya is the victim of a deep deception. Someone has lied to her; and because of this lie, she is kept under lock and key, used by her employer to service men, and indebted for the privilege. In exchange, she lives in the United States and fantasizes on a future American freedom. Or as she remarks to a friend, "Would she rather be fucking a dog . . . or living like a dog?" In Anya's world, it's a reasonable question.

Much of *I-5* transpires on the eponymous interstate. Anya travels with her "manager" and driver from Los Angeles to Oakland. It's a macabre journey: a drop at Denny's, a bad patch of fog, a visit to a "correctional facility," a rendezvous with an organ grinder, and a dramatic entry across Oakland's city limits.

"*Insightful, innovative and riveting. After its lyrical beginning inside Anya's head, I-5 shifts momentum into a rollicking gangsters-on-the-lam tale that is in turns blackly humorous, suspenseful, heartbreaking and always populated by intriguing characters. Anya is a wonderful, believable heroine, her tragic tale told from the inside out, without a shred of sentimental pity, which makes it all the stronger. A twisty, fast-paced ride you won't soon forget.*"
— Denise Hamilton, author of the *LA Times* bestseller *The Last Embrace*

"*I'm in awe. I-5 moves so fast you can barely catch your breath. It's as tough as tires, as real and nasty as road rage, and best of all, it careens at breakneck speed over as many twists and turns as you'll find on The Grapevine. What a ride! I-5's a hard-boiled standout.*"
— Julie Smith, editor of *New Orleans Noir* and author of the Skip Langdon and Talba Wallis crime novel series

"*In I-5, Summer Brenner deals with the onerous and gruesome subject of sex trafficking calmly and forcefully, making the reader feel the pain of its victims. The trick to forging a successful narrative is always in the details, and I-5 provides them in abundance. This book bleeds truth—after you finish it, the blood will be on your hands.*"
— Barry Gifford, author, poet and screenwriter

The Chieu Hoi Saloon

Michael Harris

ISBN: 978-1-60486-112-9
$19.95   376 pages

It's 1992 and three people's lives are about to
collide against the flaming backdrop of the
Rodney King riots in Los Angeles. Vietnam vet
Harry Hudson is a journalist fleeing his past:
the war, a failed marriage, and a fear-ridden
childhood. Rootless, he stutters, wrestles with
depression, and is aware he's passed the point at which victim becomes
victimizer. He explores the city's lowest dives, the only places where he
feels at home. He meets Mama Thuy, a Vietnamese woman struggling to
run a Navy bar in a tough Long Beach neighborhood, and Kelly Crenshaw,
an African-American prostitute whose husband is in prison. They give
Harry insight that maybe he can do something to change his fate in a
gripping story that is both a character study and thriller.

"Mike Harris' novel has all the brave force and arresting power of Celine and
Dostoevsky in its descent into the depths of human anguish and that peculiar
gallantry of the moral soul that is caught up in irrational self-punishment
at its own failings. Yet Harris manages an amazing and transforming
affirmation—the novel floats above all its pain on pure delight in the variety
of the human condition. It is a story of those sainted souls who live in bars,
retreating from defeat but rendered with such vividness and sensitivity that
it is impossible not to care deeply about these figures from our own waking
dreams. In an age less obsessed by sentimentality and mawkish 'uplift,' this
book would be studied and celebrated and emulated."
— John Shannon, author of *The Taking of the Waters* and the Jack Liffey
mysteries

"Michael Harris is a realist with a realist's unflinching eye for the hard truths
of contemporary times. Yet in The Chieu Hoi Saloon, he gives us a hero
worth admiring: the passive, overweight, depressed and sex-obsessed Harry
Hudson, who in the face of almost overwhelming despair still manages to
lead a valorous life of deep faith. In this powerful and compelling first novel,
Harris makes roses bloom in the gray underworld of porno shops, bars and
brothels by compassionately revealing the yearning loneliness beneath the
grime—our universal human loneliness that seeks transcendence through
love."
— Paula Huston, author of *Daughters of Song* and *The Holy Way*

Pike

Benjamin Whitmer

ISBN: 978-1-60486-089-4
$15.95   224 pages

Douglas Pike is no longer the murderous hustler he was in his youth, but reforming hasn't made him much kinder. He's just living out his life in his Appalachian hometown, working odd jobs with his partner, Rory, hemming in his demons the best he can. And his best seems just good enough until his estranged daughter overdoses and he takes in his twelve-year-old granddaughter, Wendy.

Just as the two are beginning to forge a relationship, Derrick Kreiger, a dirty Cincinnati cop, starts to take an unhealthy interest in the girl. Pike and Rory head to Cincinnati to learn what they can about Derrick and the death of Pike's daughter, and the three men circle, evenly matched predators in a human wilderness of junkie squats, roadhouse bars and homeless Vietnam vet encampments.

"Without so much as a sideways glance towards gentility, Pike *is one righteous mutherfucker of a read. I move that we put Whitmer's balls in a vise and keep slowly notching up the torque until he's willing to divulge the secret of how he managed to hit such a perfect stride his first time out of the blocks."*
— Ward Churchill

"Benjamin Whitmer's Pike *captures the grime and the rage of my not-so-fair city with disturbing precision. The words don't just tell a story here, they scream, bleed, and burst into flames.* Pike, *like its eponymous main character, is a vicious punisher that doesn't mince words or take prisoners, and no one walks away unscathed. This one's going to haunt me for quite some time."*
— Nathan Singer

"This is what noir is, what it can be when it stops playing nice—blunt force drama stripped down to the bone, then made to dance across the page."
— Stephen Graham Jones

The Wrong Thing

Barry Graham

ISBN: 978-1-60486-451-9
$14.95   136 pages

They call him the Kid. He's a killer, a dark Latino legend of the Southwest's urban badlands, "a child who terrifies adults." They speak of him in whispers in dive bars near closing time. Some claim to have met him. Others say he doesn't exist, a phantom blamed for every unsolved act of violence, a ghost who haunts every blood-splattered crime scene.

But he is real. He's a young man with a love of cooking and reading, an abiding loneliness and an appetite for violence. He is a cipher, a projection of the dreams and nightmares of people ignored by Phoenix's economic boom . . . and a contemporary outlaw in search of an ordinary life. Love brings him the chance at a new life in the form of Vanjii, a beautiful, damaged woman. But try as he might to abandon the past, his past won't abandon him. The Kid fights back in the only way he knows—and sets in motion a tragic sequence of events that lead him to an explosive conclusion shocking in its brutality and tenderness.

"Graham's words are raw and gritty, and his observations unrelenting and brutally honest."
— *Booklist*

"Graham's stories are peopled with the desperate and the mad. A master."
— *The Times*

"Vivid, almost lurid, prose. . . a talented author."
— *Time Out* (London)

Nearly Nowhere

Summer Brenner

ISBN: 978-1-60486-306-2
$15.95   192 pages

Fifteen years ago, Kate Ryan and her daughter
Ruby moved to the secluded village of Zamora
in northern New Mexico to find a quiet life off
the grid. But when Kate invites the wrong drifter
home for the night, the delicate peace of their
domain is shattered.

Troy Mason manages to hang onto Kate for a few weeks, though his
charm increasingly fails to offset his lies and delusions of grandeur. It
is only a matter of time before the lies turn abusive, igniting a chain
reaction of violence and murder. Not even a bullet in the leg will keep
Troy from seeking revenge as he chases the missing Ruby over back roads
through the Sangre de Cristo Mountains, down the River of No Return,
and to a white supremacy enclave in Idaho's Bitterroot Wilderness.
Nearly Nowhere explores the darkest places of the American West,
emerging with only a fragile hope of redemption in the maternal ties that
bind.

"*With her beautifully wrought sentences and dialogue that bring characters
alive, Summer Brenner weaves a gripping and dark tale of mysterious crime
based in spiritually and naturally rich northern New Mexico and beyond.*"
— Roxanne Dunbar-Ortiz, historian and writer, author of *Roots of
Resistance: A History of Land Tenure in New Mexico*

"*Summer Brenner's* Nearly Nowhere *has the breathless momentum of the
white-water river her characters must navigate en route from a isolated
village in New Mexico to a neo-Nazi camp in Idaho. A flawed but loving
single mother, a troubled teen girl, a good doctor with a secret, a murderous
sociopath—this short novel packs enough into its pages to fight well above
its weight class.*"
—Michael Harris, author of *The Chieu Hoi Saloon*

"*To the party, Summer Brenner brings a poet's ear, a woman's awareness,
and a soulful intent, and her attention has enriched every manner of literary
endeavor graced by it.*"
—Jim Nisbet, author of *A Moment of Doubt*

Send My Love and a Molotov Cocktail: Stories of Crime, Love and Rebellion

Edited by Gary Phillips
and Andrea Gibbons

ISBN: 978-1-60486-096-2
$19.95   368 pages

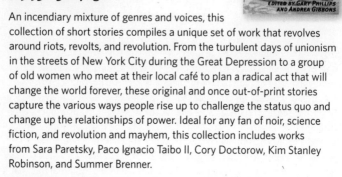

An incendiary mixture of genres and voices, this
collection of short stories compiles a unique set of work that revolves
around riots, revolts, and revolution. From the turbulent days of unionism
in the streets of New York City during the Great Depression to a group
of old women who meet at their local café to plan a radical act that will
change the world forever, these original and once out-of-print stories
capture the various ways people rise up to challenge the status quo and
change up the relationships of power. Ideal for any fan of noir, science
fiction, and revolution and mayhem, this collection includes works
from Sara Paretsky, Paco Ignacio Taibo II, Cory Doctorow, Kim Stanley
Robinson, and Summer Brenner.

Full list of contributors:

Summer Brenner
Rick Dakan
Barry Graham
Penny Mickelbury
Gary Phillips
Luis Rodriguez
Benjamin Whitmer
Michael Moorcock
Larry Fondation

Cory Doctorow
Andrea Gibbons
John A. Imani
Sara Paretsky
Kim Stanley Robinson
Paco Ignacio Taibo II
Ken Wishnia
Michael Skeet
Tim Wohlforth

The Incredible Double

Owen Hill

ISBN: 978-1-60486-083-2
$13.95   144 pages

Clay Blackburn has two jobs. Most of the time he's your average bisexual book scout in Berkeley. Some of the time he's . . . not quite a private detective. He doesn't have a license, he doesn't have a gun, he doesn't have a business card—but people come to him for help and in helping them he comes across more than his fair share of trouble. And trouble finds him seeking the fountain of youth, the myth of paradise, the pie in the sky . . . The Incredible Double.

Clay fights his way through corporate shills, Berkeley loonies, and CEO thugs on his way to understanding the secret of The Double. Follow his journey to a state of Grace, epiphanies, perhaps the meaning of life. This follow-up to *The Chandler Apartments*, red meat to charter members of the Clay Blackburn cult, is also an excellent introduction to the series. Hill brings back Blackburn's trusty, if goofy sidekicks: Marvin, best friend and lefty soldier of fortune; Bailey Dao, ex-FBI agent; Dino Centro, as smarmy as he is debonair. He also introduces a new cast of bizarre characters: drug casualty turned poet Loose Bruce, conspiracy theorist Larry Sasway, and Grace, the Tallulah Bankhead of Berkeley. Together—and sometimes not so together—they team up to foil Drugstore Wally, the CEO with an evil plan.

"Very well written, well paced, well time-lined and well-charactered. I chuckled seeing so many of my poetic acquaintances mentioned in the text."
— Ed Sanders

"Owen Hill's breathless, sly and insouciant mystery novels are full of that rare Dawn Powell-ish essence: fictional gossip. I could imagine popping in and out of his sexy little Chandler building apartment a thousand times and never having the same cocktail buzz twice. Poets have all the fun, apparently."
— Jonathan Lethem author of *The Fortress of Solitude*

"Guillaume Appollinaire and Edward Sanders would feast on this thriller of the real Berkeley and its transsexual CIA agents and doppelgangers staging Glock shoot-outs. A mystery of contingencies centering in the reeking Chandler Arms and the quicksand of Moe's Books."
— Michael McClure

Byzantium Endures: The First Volume of the Colonel Pyat Quartet

Michael Moorcock
with an introduction by Alan Wall

ISBN: 978-1-60486-491-5
$22.00   400 pages

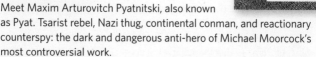

Meet Maxim Arturovitch Pyatnitski, also known as Pyat. Tsarist rebel, Nazi thug, continental conman, and reactionary counterspy: the dark and dangerous anti-hero of Michael Moorcock's most controversial work.

Published in 1981 to great critical acclaim—then condemned to the shadows and unavailable in the U.S. for thirty years—*Byzantium Endures*, the first of the Pyat Quartet, is not a book for the faint-hearted. It's the story of a cocaine addict, sexual adventurer, and obsessive anti-Semite whose epic journey from Leningrad to London connects him with scoundrels and heroes from Trotsky to Makhno, and whose career echoes that of the 20th century's descent into Fascism and total war.

This is Moorcock at his audacious, iconoclastic best: a grand sweeping overview of the events of the last century, as revealed in the secret journals of modern literature's most proudly unredeemable outlaw. This authoritative U.S. edition presents the author's final cut, restoring previously forbidden passages and deleted scenes.

"What is extraordinary about this novel. . . is the largeness of the design. Moorcock has the bravura of a nineteeth-century novelist: he takes risks, he uses fiction as if it were a divining rod for the age's most significant concerns. Here, in Byzantium Endures, *he has taken possession of the early twentieth century, of a strange, dead civilization and recast them in a form which is highly charged without ceasing to be credible."*
— Peter Ackroyd, *Sunday Times*

"A tour de force, and an extraordinary one. Mr. Moorcock has created in Pyatnitski a wholly sympathetic and highly complicated rogue. . . There is much vigorous action here, along with a depth and an intellectuality, and humor and color and wit as well."
— *The New Yorker*

"Clearly the foundation on which a gigantic literary edifice will, in due course, be erected. While others build fictional molehills, Mr. Moorcock makes plans for great shimmering pyramids. But the footings of this particular edifice are intriguing and audacious enough to leave one hungry for more."
— John Naughton, *Listener*